"Pete," she called sof
        Still no sound.
the pale light of dawn ___
windows. The Christmas tree stood where it had, the lights still
glowing.

Kim took a chance and turned on the hallway light. She
saw it immediately...several drops of blood and a tuft of orange
fluff on the carpet in front of the half-bathroom. The door was
partially open and it was dark inside.

"Pete?" Still gripping the gun in both hands, Kim pushed
the door the rest of the way open. She stepped cautiously inside
and flipped the light switch with her right elbow.

A sound came from over her head. A dry, rasping sound.
She looked toward the ceiling and nearly screamed.

There, attached to the light fixture, was some sort of
bag...or cocoon...about the size of a large purse. It seemed
to be translucent in nature. Kim thought it was made of silk
or webbing at first, but then she saw the scaly texture of the
chrysalis. Is that...is that snakeskin?

The thing revolved slowly from the leathery cable that
attached it to the fixture. It shuddered and twitched slightly,
and a soft sound came from inside.

Mew.

Kim's heart sank. Oh God! Oh, dear Jesus....

It made another lazy half-turn and stopped. That's when
she saw what was inside.

It was Sweetie-Pete.

Season's Creepings

TALES OF HOLIDAY HORROR

Creepings

BY RONALD KELLY

COPYRIGHT INFORMATION

For the Kelly kids,

Reilly, Makenna, & Ryan, for whom Christmas was always a joyful, magical, and peaceful time...except when their daddy told them gruesome yuletide ghost stories on
Christmas Eve.

CONTENTS

INTRODUCTION

Next to Halloween, Christmas has always been my favorite holiday.

In fact, in the Kelly household—both during my childhood and presently—we tend to launch into holiday mode fairly early. The rubber Wolfman mask is still flung across the couch and the Halloween candy still scattered across the kitchen counter when we break out the Christmas decorations, the six artificial trees and their totes of ornaments, and the robotic Santa Claus (which is currently on the blink and tends to sing Christmas carols and box you like Mike Tyson instead of dancing merrily as he did twenty years ago).

When I was a young'un, Christmas meant concrete ideals and traditions: the Nativity pageant at church, the shoebox under the tree with apples, oranges, mixed nuts, and tiny, foil-wrapped Santas from the big yacht-sized candy counter at the local Sears store. It also meant warm hugs and Christmas cookies from Mom, and Dad's stoic readings of *The Night Before Christmas*, Luke Chapter 2 from the Bible, and the abbreviated Classics Illustrated version of Dickens's *A Christmas Carol*. And, of course there were the TV shows: *A Charlie Brown Christmas*, *Rudolph the Red-Nosed Reindeer*, and *How the Grinch Stole Christmas!*

Then came Christmas Eve and the glorious morning afterward. Seemingly endless hours of torturous, insomnia-laden immobility as you lay in your bed, afraid to move or even breathe, in the fear that one treacherous blink of the eye might scare Saint Nicholas back up the chimney before he could accomplish his mission, leaving you sorrowfully empty-handed. But, eventually, sleep and utter emotional exhaustion would claim you and you would sleep soundly...at least until Mom poked her head through the bedroom door and said "Time to wake up! I believe Ol' Santa's been here." An Olympic-grade race down the hallway to the living room followed, then the grand reveal of the booty the Jolly One had left in our behalf. G.I. Joes (the big 12-inchers, not the 3-inch military midgets), Hot Wheels, View-Masters, Lincoln Logs, Silly Putty and Play-Doh, and Evel Knievel on his red-white-blue motorcycle...the one toy that placed your mother's frayed nerves on the precarious edge of Snake Canyon every time you revved that sucker up and let it wheelie-pop straight for things highly fragile and breakable.

Then later, when you were around ten, eleven, or twelve, the horror bug would bite you and toys no longer held the appeal they once did. And if you had really, really cool parents (uh, pardon me, I meant *Santa Claus*), the word would get around and the gifts would be more to your weird and bizarre liking. Magic trick sets, ventriloquist dummies, and weird things to decorate your torture chamber of a bedroom, like rubber shrunken heads, severed hands, and posters of the Creature from the Black Lagoon and King Kong. If you were lucky, there would be morbid reading material to provide fodder for the imagination, like copies of *Famous Monsters of Filmland* magazine and *House of Mystery* and *Werewolf By Night* comic books. Model-building kids of the weird and unconventional sort would find rattling boxes beneath the tree: Aurora monster models with glow-in-the-dark parts and the notorious and potentially serial killer-producing Monster Scenes: Doctor Deadly with his contraptions of torture, Frankenstein's Monster toting the Daisy Duke-like Victim, and, of course, the voluptuous and scantily-clad Vampirella (which most moms—mine included—treated like a skanky delinquent daughter of Satan himself, instead of a respectable and iconic vampire vixen).

It was then, during those adolescent, horror-obsessed days, that the aesthetics of both Halloween and Christmas blurred and melded almost effortlessly. Devils and angels walked hand in hand, and a magical top hat could change a mindless mound of hard-packed snowflakes into a shambling Abominable Snowman. Reindeer antlers grew razor-sharp and eager for impalement, and Santa and his trusty elves could very well be Krampus and his evil minions in search of unsuspecting children...those who might end up in next year's fruitcake or as tallow in a future Christmas candle.

I thought about strange things like that...didn't you? Probably not if you were a lover of football and mini-bikes or a maven of Barbies and Easy-Bake Ovens. But for us connoisseurs of late-night Creature Features, Boris Karloff, and creepy rubber insects from twenty-five-cent vending machines, the dark connection between horror and holiday seemed to come naturally. You could imagine that the little doorways of the advent calendar held dark prizes like spiders and severed thumbs and freshly-picked eyeballs, or that something unseen hid, brimming with mischief and malice, within the leafy green heart of the Christmas tree. You could fall asleep in your twin bed with the wagon-wheel headboard and, around midnight, awaken to wonder if the Elf on the Shelf had abandoned its post and now crawled beneath your bed, with one of Mom's sharpest filet knifes gripped in its tiny murderous hand.

The ten nightmarish tales that you are about to read come from the mind of one such imaginative youth. One who, like all boys, grew up, but in his own darkly rebellious way, never abandoned the notion that Christmas could not only be a holiday of comfort and joy, but of mind-numbing terror and soul-chilling dread...just beneath the cheerful and festive surface.

So, as you sit and read in your armchair before the crackling hearth or the twinkling lights of the Christmas tree, sipping on a warm holiday beverage, just remember, things might not be as warm and cozy as your surroundings suggest. The icy fingers of Jack Frost are but an inch from the nape of your neck and yuletide ghosts of tragic demise stand just beyond the snow-framed panes of the window, ready to come inside as soon as your eyes grow heavy and you fall drowsily into peaceful slumber...

Merry Christmas and Many Happy Holiday Nightmares!

Ronald Kelly
Brush Creek, Tennessee
October 2020

JINGLE BONES

B rennan McDonough found it during a trip to the Goodwill. It was a few days after Halloween and it was just lying there, arms and legs askew, on a shelf of decorations and costumes that people had discarded and donated after the holiday. Brennan picked up the jointed, cardboard skeleton and held it at arm's length. Its bony arms and legs unfolded and hung loosely, shifting back and forth on their rivets. It wasn't like the ones they sold now—goofy cartoon skeletons or the plastic ones at the Dollar General that had no detail to them at all. This was an old-fashioned, cardboard Halloween skeleton that resembled the anatomical chart in the examination room at the doctor's office—the three-view diagram that showed the muscles, nerves, and skeletal systems of the human body.

Brennan cupped his left hand over the pale green sternum of the skeleton and saw a faint light emanate through the gap between his forefinger and thumb. He grinned. *Glow in the dark, too!*

The twelve-year-old stared at the leering skull with the tiny hole for hanging punched through its crown. "Are you going to be my new friend?" Brennan was suddenly embarrassed that he had said it out loud. But no one was around and no one heard.

The skeleton grinned at him with those pearly teeth and black, eyeless sockets. *"You bet, buddy!"* he seemed say. *"I've got your back!"*

His back. As he lowered the cardboard decoration and began to fold its arms and legs across its torso, Brennan grimaced at the soreness that ran, in intervals, down the length of his back, from just beneath his shoulder blades to the tops of his thighs. Just thinking about it made the boy feel both angry and ashamed. He remembered his stepfather Stu's hand trailing down his naked body in the downstairs bathroom. There had been nothing sexual about it at all...he had only been mapping out where his size 52 belt would apply the lashes. All because he had forgotten to lower the garage door after coming in from raking the front yard leaves.

Brennan tucked the skeleton under his arm and went to find his mother. He found Peggy McDonough—now Peggy Compton—in an aisle of battered purses that looked like they'd barely survived a hurricane. "Mom?"

Mom frowned as she studied a Louis Vuitton purse that turned out to be a cheap knockoff. "Hmmm? What is it, dear?"

"Can I get this?"

The thin woman with honey-blond hair and glasses glanced over at him. Her frown grew more severe. "Halloween's over and done with, Bren."

"But...but I could hang him on my door and decorate him for different holidays," he told her, searching for a good reason. "It doesn't have to be for Halloween."

"I don't know...Stu gets kind of pissed when I spend too much money."

Brennan felt his ears redden. *Well, it's your money... not his!* He thought of his lousy stepfather and how difficult it had been for the past four years. A lazy, worthless, overweight man in his mid-forties that reigned over them like a prison warden and wasn't past slapping or strapping either one of them if he didn't get his way, or if anything set him off. Numerous times, Brennan had wanted to ask his mother *Why did you marry him?* or *Why do you let him beat the crap out of me?* But he never had and probably never would. His dad's death had been hard on both of them, but particularly so for his mom. She had worried herself crazy over how they were going to pay the bills and make it from day to day, until she finally agreed to date Stu Compton and eventually married him. From the moment she had said "I do" at the county courthouse, they hadn't enjoyed an easy day. Stu had turned out to be a monster—a childish bully of a man who enjoyed humiliating his new family, with both words and violence.

"I've got a few dollars Grandma gave me for my birthday," Brennan told her. "I swear, I'll pay you back as soon as we get home."

His mom thought about it for a moment. "Okay...just make sure you do."

Brennan grinned from ear to ear. *You're going home with me, Bones!* the boy thought.

The skeleton grinned back gleefully. *I'm with you all the way, pal!*

The month of November was a rough one for Brennan.

Stu had been particularly vicious that month for some reason. He was spending too much bill money on beer and lottery cards and, when collection agencies began to call the house or the checking account got overdrawn, the man grew agitated and irritable. In turn, Stu would take it all out on Peggy and Brennan. He had punched his wife in the side so hard during the second week of November that she'd suffered sore ribs and a fist-sized bruise that turned an ugly yellowish-purple. Of course, she refused to see a doctor and no one had seen it but Brennan...and that had been by accident, when he walked by her bedroom door and saw her examining the place in the mirror with tears in her eyes.

Brennan had tried his best to stay out of Stu's way, hiding out in his room as much as possible. He hung the Goodwill skeleton on his closet door and, sneaking paper from his mother's scrapbooking supplies, made him a pilgrim outfit, complete with the high-peaked hat with the buckle on the front. He even drew an old-fashioned blunderbuss and taped it to his skeletal hand. Bones grinned at him, looking like he would have winked...if he'd had eyelids. *I'd do it for you*, his new friend seemed to say. *I'd put a load of lead right in that fat bastard's sorry ass! Just give me the word!*

But attempting to dodge Stu was impossible most of the time. He locked Brennan in the closet from suppertime until breakfast several times, just for stupid little goofs or mistakes that didn't amount to much. And he took the belt to him once or twice, too. The boy's dislike and fear for his stepfather slowly turned to outright hatred. Sometimes at night, as he lay in bed on his stomach with the whelps on his back inflamed and stinging, Brennan couldn't help but cry, burying his face in his pillow so Stu wouldn't hear. He thought of his dad and cried even more. *Why did you have to die, Dad?* he would wonder. *Why did you have to fall off that scaffold and break your neck…and leave us to deal with him?*

Across the room, on the closet door, Bones hung there in the darkness, outlined in that eerie green glow of his. He smiled that perpetual toothy grin, as if saying *I'm here for you, Brennan. Right down to the very end, buddy.*

It was the last week in November when the school bully, Troy Anderson, nailed him hard in the back during dodgeball in the gym. The pain had been so intense that Brennan had fallen to his hands and knees, scarcely able to breathe. One of the teachers—Mrs. Holden from his home room—had seen his distress and helped him up, while the PE teacher had laughed with the others.

When she had led him to the outer hallway, she touched his lower back and he cried out. Despite his protest, she lifted his shirt and saw the ugly marks across his back. "Let's go talk to the principal," she suggested. "Something has got to be done about this."

"No!" Brennan protested. "I'm okay. Let's just forget about it. Please?"

But Mrs. Holden wouldn't be dissuaded. "This is very serious, Brennan. Now, let's go."

When the principal, Coach Meechum, walked out of his office, raised the back of the middle-schooler's shirt, and examined the stripes on his back, he said "Hmmm…okay. Brennan, why don't you sit in the conference room there. I'm going to call your parents."

"Just call my mom, please," the boy blurted.

A little smile crossed the principal's beefy face. "Just have a seat and we'll get to the bottom of this."

Sitting in the conference room, Brennan knew this wasn't

going to turn out well. To tell the truth, he hated Coach Meechum about as much as he did Stu… maybe even more. It wasn't because Bob Meechum was a redneck asshole of a football coach who had been granted the additional power of being principal. No, it had to do more with his daughter, Emily. Emily Meechum, a small, quiet girl that pretty much kept to herself, was in Brennan's seventh-grade class. Perhaps it was a mutual sadness—or a shared desperation—that had forged their friendship. Sometimes, during lunch, Brennan sat with her at a table to themselves. They would talk about books and video games and old horror movies they both liked. Once, she had grown quiet and begun crying. She told him things about her dad…about why she hated nighttime and wished that she had a lock on her bedroom door.

Brennan had wanted to tell her about Stu and the beatings, but was afraid she wouldn't be his friend anymore if she discovered that he was just as broken as she was.

He sat in the conference room for a half hour before the door finally opened. When it did, Coach Meechum and Stu Compton walked in.

"Where's my mother?" he asked them. "Where's Mrs. Holden?"

"Your mom couldn't leave work," the principal told him flatly. "As for Mrs. Holden, she had classes to attend to. She's a teacher, Brennan. That's what she gets paid for. Not being a crusader or an advocate."

"So, what seems to be the problem?" asked Stu. He sat down in a chair directly across the table from his stepson. Leaning back, he smiled at the boy.

"A teacher was concerned," Meechum told him. "About his back."

Stu seemed puzzled. "His back?"

"I know you too well, Stu," said the coach…and he did. Not only were they neighbors—the Meechums lived across the street from them—but Bob and Stu had gone to high school together and played on the same football team. "Sure, you can get a little hot-headed and impulsive. But I know what happened was probably justified. That it was simply a little old-fashioned woodshed discipline between a dad and his son."

"Discipline?" Brennan was scared to death. He felt cornered, alone in the room with the two men in the world that he despised most, but the absurdity of the coach's statement just made him blurt it out. "He took a belt and beat me!"

Coach Meechum shook his big, crew-cut head. "Now, Brennan...that word...*beat*...it's such an ugly word. The kind of word that gets people all emotional. No, I think the other word is more appropriate in this situation. *Discipline*...that is what I should classify this as in my report."

Stu seemed surprised. "Report? Is that really necessary, Bob?"

"Buddy, if it was up to me...no. But times have changed since we were in school. There's accountability for everything. Mrs. Holden is all out to save your boy's poor, bruised little ass. She's ready to call in Child Protective Services. We don't want that to happen, do we? So we've got to work together to pacify Mrs. Holden and the school board."

"What do you suggest, Bob?"

"I know the boy probably deserved what he got, but go a little easier on him," the principal advised. "There must be other—less obvious—ways to discipline a kid without getting folks all upset."

Stu laughed. It was an ugly sound. "You know what the Bible says. Spare the rod...spoil the child."

"Oh, I'm well aware of that," Coach Meechum said. A thin smile crossed his massive face. "My daughter, Emily...she gets the rod every now and then, too."

Brennan's hatred at that moment was so palatable that he felt that it might catch fire and consume him. The two men who kindled that rage didn't even seem to notice.

"Okay," said Stu with a shrug and a sigh. "He's a forgetful and unruly kid, but I'll go easy on him from now on. Or, at least, I'll try."

"That's all I ask," said the principal. "I'll call Mrs. Holden into my office later...have a nice, long talk with her. Convince her that dropping this whole thing is in Brennan's best interest."

"I'd appreciate that, pal." Stu stood up and shook the principal's hand firmly.

"It's only an hour until school lets out and it's Friday,"

Meechum said. "Why don't you go ahead and sign Brennan out. Take him home...have a little father-and-son bonding time before Peggy gets home from work."

"Sounds like a plan." As Brennan walked around the table, Stu clapped him heartily on the back, bringing a fresh burst of pain. "Come on, son."

The drive home had been a long and silent one. Brennan sat in the passenger seat, as far against the door as he could manage. Stu whistled and smiled as he drove, as though he didn't have a care in the world...or was planning something in the back of his head.

The moment they entered the house, with the front door closed behind them, it happened. Brennan felt himself nearly propelled off his feet as he was shoved forcefully from behind. He ended up, face-first, in the foyer wall...so hard that it bloodied his nose. Then Stu was there, twisting his arm behind his back and breathing in his ear.

"I told you to never tell, didn't I?" he said, leaning forward and sandwiching the twelve-year-old between his bulk and the wall. "I told you what I'd do to you and your mother if anyone found out and started sticking their nose in our business."

"I...I didn't tell!" shrieked Brennan. The pressure was so crushing that he could scarcely breathe. "My teacher just found out, that's all! I didn't tell her anything!"

"You're lying, you little chickenshit!" Stu's massive hand encircled the nape of Brennan's neck. "I oughta snap your freaking spine for what I had to put up with today."

Tears mingled with the blood between Brennan's face and the wall. "Don't! Please...please, just leave me alone!"

"Alone?" Stu laughed harshly. "You want to be alone? Well, come on...you can be alone all weekend."

As Stu grabbed his arm and dragged him down the hallway, Brennan tried anything in his power to stop him—dug his heels into the carpet, clung tightly to nearby furniture...anything to slow his progress. "Please, Stu...don't! I don't want to go in there!"

A moment later, they were there...in front of Brennan's

bedroom closet. He had thought it strange when Stu and his mom had first married...Stu installing the deadbolt on the *outside* of his closet the way he did. But, afterward, he discovered it was for a very disturbing reason.

"No, Stu! Please!" he pleaded. "I'll be good! I promise I will!"

"Of course you will," Stu told him. "Locked in here for the weekend. No food, no water."

His stepfather reached for the doorknob of the closet, then stopped. He stared at the Halloween skeleton on the door—all smiles, his hinged arms and legs splayed here and there, as though he were dancing happily. He still had on the pilgrim outfit and held the blunderbuss. From the flared muzzle of the gun was an exaggerated puff of smoke that read "BOOM! You're dead!"

"Damn skeleton!" Stu shoved Brennan to the floor, then tore the decoration from where it was pinned to the door. The boy watched angrily as Stu went furiously to work, first tearing Bones in half at the lower spine, then dismembering his arms and legs, and finally decapitating the grinning skull from its neck bone. Pieces of cardboard skeleton lay scattered across the bedroom floor as Stu grabbed Brennan by the collar of his jacket and tossed him into the closet with such force that the top of his head slammed into the back wall.

Then, abruptly, the door closed and, except for a narrow sliver of light underneath, there was only darkness,. The deadbolt engaged with a heavy *clack*. Brennan knew from experience that he wouldn't hear it disengage until Sunday evening. He backpedaled into a corner of his solitary confinement and sat there with his injured back against the cool drywall.

Later that evening, when his mother got home from work, there was an argument. It didn't last very long. Brennan flinched as he heard the ugly sounds of fists on flesh and his mother's crying. Stu yelled some more and then retired to the living room to watch *Wheel of Fortune* and the evening news before suppertime.

A few hours passed. The house had settled down. It was quiet, only the sound of the television playing. Brennan looked down and saw something being slipped beneath the closet door. It was a slice of peanut butter toast.

Brennan took the food and devoured it hungrily. "Mom... Mom, let me out."

Peggy Compton paused, then sighed. "I can't, sweetheart."

"Mom, we've got to get out of here. We've got to leave."

"We can't do that, Bren. We don't have any choice."

"Yes, we do!" he cried. "Mom...please. He's going to lose his temper and end up killing one of us. Maybe me and you both."

His mother was silent for a long moment. "I'm sorry, son. I...I just can't."

Then her shadow at the base of the door vanished and she was gone.

It was a little after midnight when Brennan heard someone outside the closet door.

The boy sat up abruptly from where he had been curled on the floor, beneath a winter coat he had pulled off a hanger. His heart pounded as the doorknob jiggled, followed by the crisp, metallic snap of the deadbolt disengaging.

He expected Stu to burst in and whale into him, with his fist or his belt. But no one even opened the door. Brennan sat there, scared, for five minutes or more, before he finally mustered the courage to creep forward and try the door himself. The knob turned freely and the door swung outward into darkness.

Brennan stood up and stepped into his bedroom. It was cool that night—in the mid-fifties—and he couldn't help but shiver. As he turned and closed the closet door, he was startled to find the outline of the glow-in-the-dark skeleton hanging on the upper door panel where it had been before. Its bones blazed in eerie green relief against the black of night.

The boy reached out curiously. Had Stu or Mom taped him back together and pinned him on the door? His fingers felt along the skeleton's neck and the vertebrae of his lower spine. He could find no evidence of tape or glue. It was as though the cardboard had healed itself.

"What are we going to do, Bones?" he whispered softly. "How are we going to get through this?"

The skeleton grinned down at him, as if saying *Don't worry, buddy. We'll get through this together. I promise. Just be patient.*

Brennan reached out and took Bone's hand for a moment,
then let it swing free. He crawled into his bed, snuggled
beneath the covers, and fell asleep.

Brennan dreaded the approach of Christmas...mostly because
Santa Claus had broken his arm in two places the year before.

He remembered it well. He had fallen asleep on Christmas
Eve and was sleeping peacefully, when he awoke in the night.
Someone was in his room. He sat up in bed and saw a massive
silhouette against his moonlit window. "*Ho, ho, ho,*" Stu whispered.
Then he loomed over him, dressed in the whole outfit: red suit,
beard, the fur-rimmed cap with the fuzzy ball on the end.

Brennan had felt Santa's hands enclose his left forearm. "I'm
sick of you interfering, you little turd. Mouthing off when me and
your mom are having one of our *discussions.* Time to teach you a
lesson...make you remember that your mother is *mine* now, not
that maggot hotel of a daddy that's rotting six feet under."

The boy recalled the awful pressure and pain as Stu began to
bend. "Here's the story and you sure as hell better remember it for
anyone who asks. You got up to pee and tripped in the bathroom.
Fell and hit your arm on the edge of the tub. Do you understand?"

"Please," Brennan had whimpered. "Please, don't...."

"Do...you...*understand*?"

Brennan had nodded. Then came the splintering *crack* and the
screams. *His* screams. A moment later, his mother ran into the
room, bundled him up, and drove him to the emergency room.

He thought of that as he decorated the skeleton for Christmas.
Carefully, he removed the pilgrim outfit and replaced it with a
Santa suit of red construction paper and cotton balls from his
mom's bathroom. It was only half a suit, ending at the waist,
sort of like the Grinch's. There was no beard to the ensemble. It
seemed a shame to cover the skeleton's cheerful, grinning face.

"I'm christening you Jingle Bones for the holidays," he said
aloud.

Sounds great to me, Bren! the skeleton seemed to reply. Take it
from me, kid, this is gonna be the best Christmas ever! Just you
wait and see!

"Yeah, right," Brennan said sadly. "We can dream, can't we?"

Jingle Bones just grinned, as if knowing what lay ahead, but refusing to spill the beans.

The next three weeks went by fast. There were no arguments, no hateful remarks, no punishments. Stu almost seemed to have changed overnight. He was jovial and easy to get along with, and had even helped put up and decorate the tree, and strung lights along the gutters and eaves of the house. At night, they sat in the living room like a real family, drinking eggnog and eating Christmas cookies, and watching old movies like *It's a Wonderful Life* and *Miracle on 34th Street.*

Brennan should have found comfort in that, the sudden wellspring of peace and joy that the household experienced. But he didn't. All he felt was suspicion and an underlying dread that he couldn't quite explain. He knew Stu and what he was capable of…probably more than his mother did. Brennan was convinced that Stu was still the sadistic bastard he had always been.

He just had something planned for later on…something up his sleeve. Something bad.

It happened on Christmas Eve night, just like it had before.

They had enjoyed a nice, quiet evening around the Christmas tree, listening to holiday music and wrapping gifts. Brennan and his mom had set out milk and cookies for Santa, even though he was beyond the age of believing. When Mom had tucked Brennan in and kissed him goodnight, it was like old times again. He drifted to sleep with the hope that maybe… just *maybe*…this would turn out to be a nice Christmas after all.

Then, around one o'clock on Christmas morning, a horrible sensation of pressure across his right thigh woke him up in a panic. Before he could cry out, a meaty hand clamped tightly over his mouth.

"Merry Christmas, Brennan," Stu said, his voice slightly muffled by the curly, white beard.

"Get off of me!" the boy tried to say, but it only came out as garbled mumbling.

"So, what are we going to do this year?" the big man hissed

in the darkness. His knee bore deeply into the muscle just above Brennan's knee. "How about the leg? A broken femur that'll lay you up for the winter...maybe longer. Yeah, that's what Ol' Santa will bring you this year. This time you were sleepwalking. Fell down the cellar stairs." Stu's other hand reached out and caressed the crown of Brennan's head. "Better add a skull fracture for good measure, just to make the whole thing look kosher."

Tears bloomed in the twelve-year-old's eyes as he stared up at the monster in Santa's clothing.

Stu read the question in Brennan's eyes. "Why? Because I hate you, you little shit. I never wanted you in the equation from the beginning. Who knows...maybe the concussion will do you in. Maybe when I snap your leg in half, your femoral artery will puncture and you'll bleed to death. Then I'll have your mother all to myself."

Brennan began to struggle as Stu rocked forward, pressing all of his weight against the boy's leg. At the same time, the man doubled his right fist—which looked as massive and destructive as a sledgehammer—and brought it overhead, to come crashing down on his skull.

But it never happened.

The pressure against Brennan's thigh suddenly lessened as Stu straightened and arched backward. A dull thud sounded, followed by a moist noise like something sharp sliding cleanly through fat and meat, and a gritty, grating sound like steel against bone. Despite the darkness in the room, Brennan could see the agony and horror in Stu Compton's eyes.

And he saw something else. Or *thought* he saw.

Something entwined around Stu's throat. Something eerily green and glowing. Something that resembled the humerus, radius, and ulna of a skeletal arm.

Frightened, Brennan ducked beneath the covers and squeezed his eyes shut. A struggle took place in the bedroom. Staggering steps as a man attempted to regain his footing, a choking and wheezing as precious air was cut off and deprived, and that ugly sound of a knife blade, honed and able, doing its wet work.

Then there was a tremendous crash that seemed to shake the entire house. Brennan lay there quietly, breathing shallowly, listening. He heard a sound like someone dragging something incredibly heavy across the bedroom floor and into the hallway beyond.

The boy must have laid there, beneath the covers, for ten or fifteen minutes, before he finally gathered the nerve to poke his head out. He saw two things. First, the bedroom door was standing open with the faint multi-colored glow of the Christmas tree drifting from the far end of the outer hallway. And secondly, the front of his closet door was bare and empty. Nothing hung there at all.

Slowly, he slipped from beneath the blanket and walked, barefooted, to the bedroom door. Across the hall, the door to the master bedroom was open. He saw his mother sleeping soundly. She hadn't heard a sound.

From the direction of the living room echoed soft Christmas music. An old favorite of his mother's...Burl Ives singing "A Holly Jolly Christmas."

Brennan's curiosity outweighed his fear. He left his bedroom and started down the hallway. When he reached the living room, he found the lights on the Christmas tree twinkling and a warm and comforting fire blazing in the hollow of the fireplace.

Someone dressed in a Santa suit was stooping next to the tree, placing brightly-wrapped presents from a great, brown leather bag.

"Stu?" he asked softly. Maybe it had all been a joke...or only a nightmare. Maybe his stepfather had changed in some unexpected and wonderful way.

Santa Claus turned around. It was Stu...and it *wasn't* Stu.

The thing that stood before him had Stu's broad, double-chinned face, but there were things wrong about it. It was loose and slightly off-kilter, as though the structure underneath could hardly support the weight of the flesh. The sagging eyeholes were empty and dark. Black pits with no eyeballs whatsoever. The massive body beneath the Santa suit was the same, slack and hanging in great folds and rolls, like the waxy drippings of a candle.

Santa lifted a hand with drooping, dangling fingers and pointed to the big leather La-Z-Boy next to the fireplace. A large skeleton, bloody and scarred from defleshing, sat there casually. There was a butcher knife from Mom's kitchen drawer buried in the center of the skeleton's sternum. The eyes that still sat in the gory sockets of the silently screaming skull were grayish-blue... just like Stu's.

After Santa had finished his work, he walked over to the recliner, began to disassemble the bones, and chuck them into his empty sack. He pried the knife from Stu's breastbone and buried it, point-first, into the arm of the easy chair. Then he waved at Brennan and turned toward the door.

"Jingle Bones?"

The sagging, shambling Santa turned at the boy's voice and stared at him.

"Emily deserves a Merry Christmas, too."

Both Brennan and Jingle Bones looked through the big picture window beyond the Christmas tree. Across the snowy lawn, beyond the plowed and salted street, stood the Meechum house. A light glowed in the living room window and, through the curtains, they both saw the silhouette of a man heading toward the far end of the house...where Brennan knew his friend's bedroom was located.

Jingle Bones opened his borrowed mouth with a big, loose-lipped smile. Inside the orifice shone the skeleton's perfect, pearly teeth. They grinned gleefully, glowing gruesomely green in the cave of Stu's lower face.

Anything you say, buddy! Jingle Bones seemed to say with a nod of his head. He walked back to the chair, extracted the butcher knife from the arm, and slid it into the broad, black belt of his Santa suit.

Brennan stood in the festive living room, his youthful heart brimming with excitement and holiday cheer. There were dozens of gifts beneath the tree, a warm and cozy fire crackling in the hearth, and a murderous Santa trudging through the snow to deliver a little yuletide justice to Coach Meechum.

Jingle Bones had been right.

It looked like it was going to be one helluva Christmas after all.

THE SKATING POND

It first happened to my brother Willie.

Chilton's Pond was the best spot for ice skating in Murphy County, perhaps the best in all Tennessee. Whenever a sparse flurry swept the wooded hills and hollows, all the kids along the rural stretch of Copper Creek Road prayed that it might grow into a solid snowfall, that a deep freeze would follow, changing the oval cow pond into a skater's delight. After a half-dozen inches of fresh powder had settled upon the vacant fields of the Chilton farm and the temperature had dipped below the teens, its brackish waters would solidify into an icy surface as flat and smooth as the face of a mirror.

It was like that on that snowy Christmas morning in 1993. Willie was eleven then and I was just a month or so past the age of eight. Playing with new toys and helping Mom bake sugar cookies had gradually lost its appeal. We grew restless, knowing that the pond was waiting. Finally, after sufficient begging on our part, Mom gave us her okay and we set off down the road for the old Chilton place.

Leon Chilton knew us to be polite, well-mannered boys, so he nodded his approval and, with a hoot and a holler, we ran across the pasture to where the twisted black claw of an ancient sassafras tree stood sentry over the sixty-foot pond. We scrambled through the snowy thicket of brush and blackberry bramble that grew heavy on the southern side, then stood breathing heavily on the bank, half out of exhaustion, half out of unrestrained awe. The pond was beautiful. The cold afternoon sun glistened on its frigid surface, causing the icicles on the branches of the old tree to sparkle like diamond fangs.

"Last one on the ice is a rotten egg!" Willie said. He sat on an exposed root, shucking his shoes and tugging on the new skates he had received from Santa that morning.

"I forgot mine," I moaned. I had left my skates on Old Man Chilton's back porch. "Gotta go back. Wait for me, you hear?"

"Wait like heck!" Willie gave me a sneering grin. "I'm outta here!" And, with that, he glided out onto the slick hardness of virgin ice.

It took me a good five minutes to run back, grab my skates, and return to the pond. By the time I reached the undergrowth, a nagging pain stitched my side from running too fast. I found an old hickory stump and sat down to rest. While I sat picking at a stubborn knot in my boot laces, I could hear Willie out on the pond, whistling, the blades of his skates making swishing sounds as he performed figure-eights and hands-behind-the-back squatting glides from one end of the outdoor rink to the other.

"Hold your horses, Willie... I'm coming!" I remember yelling... just before the crack.

The sound was so sudden, so sinisterly brittle, that I was frozen to that stump. It was unmistakable and, at once, I knew exactly what had happened. The ice had broken... split beneath Willie's weight as he moved over a weak spot in the frozen pond.

I sat there for a long moment after the crackle of shattered ice, waiting breathlessly for other sounds to follow, the liquid splash as Willie plunged into the cold water underneath and his screams for help. But I swear to God, I heard nothing. Nothing but that gunshot report of thin ice giving way.

Tossing my skates aside, I tore through the brush, my heart pounding in my chest. I ran along the shallow bank, tripping over stones and frozen cow-pies, calling Willie's name. My panic grew into a numb confusion, because, no matter where I looked, I could see no visible opening in Chilton's Pond. There was no jagged crack of exposed water, just a silky smooth surface of solid ice, blemished only by a few swipes from a pair of new skates. But that wasn't what alarmed me right off. It was the total absence of sound or motion that made my blood run cold.

The skating pond was empty. My brother was nowhere to be seen.

I was scared plumb out of my wits for a minute. Then I figured I had been suckered by one of Willie's practical jokes. "Come on, Willie!" I pleaded. "This ain't funny. Come on out and let's skate!"

The pond stared at me silently like a huge glass eye. The thicket rattled to my right and I turned angrily, expecting to see my older brother standing there with a big grin on his freckled face. But it was only a winter cardinal. The red bird flew out of the bramble, lit for a second on a corkscrew limb of the sassafras, then winged his way southward toward the open fields.

Spooked, I ran for the Chilton house. Leon was in the barn with his son, Jasper, who was a high-school dropout and as dim-witted as a bullfrog.

"What in tarnation is the matter with you, boy?" the old man asked.

My breathing was so labored that I could only point wordlessly toward the pond. The three of us piled into Leon's Ford pickup and headed across the snowy pasture. We searched the thicket around the little pond, but it was empty. No mischievous boy hiding there, stifling giggles at such a great prank. Nothing but snow-laden honeysuckle and frozen cocklebur.

Then, when the old man and his son were on the other side of the pond, I just happened to glance down at the ice and thought I saw... well, that's the problem. I can't for the life of me remember what I saw. I sort of fainted, and when I awoke I was in my bedroom at home, hearing my mother's hysterical weeping drifting from the parlor downstairs and my father's useless comforting.

My brother was never found. I don't really remember much about the awful days afterward. I recall my mother lying bedridden with grief, my father standing for hours on end on the front porch, staring off toward the Chilton place, and the posters in all the shop windows in town displaying Willie's fifth-grade class picture and a $1000 reward. And I recall the county sheriff asking me a lot of strange questions, like "Did you see any strangers hanging around the pond?"

After the interrogation, the word "runaway" was

mentioned... a label pinned on my missing brother for the
sake of clearing up an incident that had no logical explanation.
I tried to tell them about the loud crack I had heard, but they
ignored me. After all, there had been no such break in the neat,
unblemished surface of Chilton's Pond.

Those terrible memories of that winter day must have
gradually lost their impact with the passage of time, for, if
they had retained their clarity, perhaps it wouldn't have
happened again... some twenty years later.

My two children loved ice skating. They were much younger
than I had been when I first started. Kevin was seven and little
Kelly was five and a half. All they had ever known was the big
indoor rink in the city, so I thought it would be a real treat for
them to skate on an old-fashioned outdoor pond. If I had only
known that our little trip into the country would end in tragedy,
I would have given their skates to the Salvation Army and for-
bidden them from the sport. But with age, my youthful recollec-
tions had dulled and so we went.

It was overcast that December morning five years ago, when,
hand in hand, I led my son and daughter across the field to
Chilton's Pond. It looked exactly as it had that day so many years
before. The children broke away in excitement. They were at the
pond's edge and already had their skates on by the time I caught
up to them. "Come on, Daddy!" little Kelly called. She took her
brother's hand as they stepped onto the newly-hardened ice.

"Just let me lace up and I'll be there, honey." I removed my
shoes and tugged at the knot that linked my skates together.
A smile crossed my face as I heard them laughing happily, the
sounds of steel against ice nearing, then ebbing as they leisurely
circled the length and breadth of the tiny pond.

I was about to slip my feet into the boots, when I heard it.

Crack!

This time no thicket obscured my view. My eyes flashed
from the frozen ground at my feet, across Chilton's Pond. There
was indeed a crack in the pond this time, a very large split at the
very far end. But I could see neither child. Wait... I did see—that
is I *thought* I saw—one mittened hand protruding, outstretched,

from beneath the level of the ice. Then it sank and was gone.

I ran, screaming and in stocking feet, across the cold surface of the skating pond. When I got there, I found the hole to be much smaller than it first looked. "Kevin! Kelly!" I screamed, staring down into the dark, swirling water. I could see nothing down there. I was about to shed my fur-collared parka and plunge in after them, when something peculiar happened.

The ice at the lip of the crack seemed to be *reforming*. In horror, I watched as the opening shrank to the size of a matter of feet, then mere inches. Then, with a brittle *pop*, the ice had completely healed itself.

After that, everything seems a blur. I remember running to the Chilton house, returning to the pond with Jasper, armed with nylon rope and blankets. I remember having a violent argument with John Reed, the Murphy County sheriff, about what had taken place. "But there ain't no break in the ice," he kept saying. "It closed up," I tried to tell him. "It refroze or something… but they're down there!" The sheriff and Jasper were exchanging doubtful glances, when I again happened to look down at the ice and saw…

They tell me I had a nervous breakdown. I don't remember much of anything, just as before when I was a kid. There are disturbing images of my wife Jessica coming at me in an awful rage, clawing at my eyes, calling me a "murdering bastard!" There are other images of a clean, white place, where men in bathrobes roamed like zombies, strung out on Thorazine… shades of *One Flew Over the Cuckoo's Nest*. After three years, I began to resurface from my dark journey of the mind… began to come to terms with the impossibility of what I thought I had seen that horrible winter day.

They released me in 2018. I was diagnosed as a paranoid schizophrenic, but of no real harm to anyone… if I remained on medication. I discovered on the day of my liberation that I had nothing to return to. My career as an architect was shot and Jessica had divorced me six months after my commitment, taking every security, every bit of property. I took to the streets and became one of the homeless. But when winter rolled around, I did not flock to the downtown shelters with all the others. Instead, I hitched a ride into the country... back to Murphy County.

I walked the rural backroads until I came to the Chilton property. It had come a big snowfall the day before and an overnight freeze had solidified the pond. A few children were there, laughing and skating the day away. Something inside me snapped. I threw my pack aside and ran toward them, waving my arms, yelling incoherently. Terrified, they ran home.

Jasper Chilton defended me when the sheriff came out to check reports of a psycho out at Chilton's Pond. "He ain't out to harm no one," Jasper had told him. Sheriff Reed was not so sure. The constable had always suspected that I had killed my own children, although he never had any physical evidence to prove it. Jasper told me that a year after I went to the asylum, the lawman and his deputies had dragged the pond during the spring, just on the unlikely chance that there might actually be bodies there. But all they had dredged from the bottom mud with their hooks and lines was an old water trough and a hunk of innertube.

Jasper gave me a job doing chores around the place, more out of pity than anything else. I promised not to bother the children again and he took me at my word. I do my work well, my thoughts drifting only when snow clouds crowd the Tennessee sky like mats of dirty cotton and the weatherman predicts freezing temperatures. Jasper never scolds me when I wander from my chores and stand, staring, at the cow pond, watching the winter breeze crystallize the murky water. Sometimes I stay there all night, just watching, knowing that the morning will bring the sound of children's laughter and the steely clink of skates slung across youthful shoulders.

And, sometimes, when the moonlight strikes the pond just right, I can see them staring up at me from cold waters... tiny, bloated faces with dead, fish eyes... and I scream and stomp on the frozen surface with the fury of a madman.

But the ice holds firm.

DEPRAVITY ROAD

"We're lost."

Fred Barnett didn't want to admit it, not out loud, not in front of *her*, but there was simply no denying it. They had been on that lonely stretch of snowy rural road for quite some time now, driving mile upon mile without seeing any signs of civilization other than a few dilapidated farmhouses and their equally ramshackle outbuildings.

"I told you that an hour ago," huffed Agnes from the passenger side of the '51 Chevrolet. "I shouldn't be surprised, though. Leave it to you to turn a simple ninety-mile road trip into some rambling exodus into the unknown. I swear, Fred, you couldn't find your own ass if you had a compass and a roadmap."

Fred's thin face flushed red with embarrassment. "Please, Agnes... not in front of the kids."

But his wife wouldn't leave it alone. "And why not in front of the kids?" she asked. "They have as much a right as anyone else to know what a total idiot their father is."

As usual, Fred said nothing in rebuttal. He avoided looking at the woman seated next to him, the woman he had once seriously thought of in terms of love, devotion, and, God help him, even lust. He didn't want to see her hefty, thick-limbed frame perched there, punishing the springs of the Chevy's two-toned bench seat. Neither did he want to see the look of smug disapproval on her plump, bovine face. Instead he directed his nervous gaze at the rearview mirror. The children, two boys named Teddy and Roger, sat immersed in their comic books, oblivious to the humiliation their old man was suffering at the razor tongue of their overbearing mother. Or maybe they did hear what was being said and were just ignoring it. They had heard it all many times before. Perhaps burying their noses in pulp pages of ballooned dialogue and brightly inked panels was a way out for them. A method of psychological escape to keep themselves from going totally nuts.

Fred wished he possessed such a haven, but he did not. Since marrying Agnes eight years ago, the shoe salesman had been unable to find one. Every waking hour was spent on the battle line, bitterly swallowing one complaint after another: dissatisfaction over the meager wage Fred was making, putting down the Eisenhower administration (Agnes did not "like Ike"), and griping because the boys were turning out to be a couple of "weird deadbeats" like their father. Of course, Fred simply nodded obediently to every harsh word, uttered a much practiced "Yes, dear," and cowered beneath her contemptuous glare, which was set in her massive face like two tiny black marbles sunk deep into a tub of lard.

Now he was under the oppressive weight of her wrath once again as he wandered the wintry backroads with no idea where they were. "Got any suggestions?" he asked her, trying desperately hard to keep the sarcasm out of his voice. "You know I've never been to your brother Ben's place before. I've never even been this far north in the state."

Agnes seemed to settle down a bit, accepting her husband's shortcomings as a burden that must be endured, at least on that Christmas Day of 1954. "Just keep on going and, the next house you see, stop and ask for directions."

"Yes, dear." There was no feeling to his words. They were just a reflex action now, like flinching beneath the fist of a bully.

Fred drove on. Miles of desolate farmland passed on either side of the narrow, snow-packed road. Some of it was vacant fields already past the time of harvest, some of it dense pine wood and marsh. There was such an air of despair and hopelessness about the area. It was a land that knew no prosperity, no joy, and no fighting chance of being anything but what it was forever destined to be—a bleak and colorless wasteland.

A land as lifeless as the territory of Fred's own floundering spirit.

Agnes sucked on the lemon drops she had bought before leaving Milwaukee and fiddled with the knobs on the radio until a Hank Williams song blared from the speaker. Teddy and Roger giggled and gasped over their comics and slurped from near-empty bottles of Nehi Grape bought at a little mom-and-pop grocery thirty miles back.

And Fred drove... and drove and drove.

Finally, something showed itself amid the snowy fields and rampant forest. A lonely farmhouse stood a hundred yards from the edge of the roadway, along with a scattering of rickety buildings: a barn, chicken coop, and outhouse. He didn't slow down at first, though, simply for the reason that the place looked totally abandoned. No vehicles sat in the driveway, the windows of the house looked dark and curtained, and what few pieces of farm machinery remained in the yard looked as though they had rusted into uselessness long ago.

But Agnes wasn't so easily convinced. "Stop!" she demanded, placing a meaty hand on his slender arm.

"Looks like the place is deserted, dear. I don't think anyone lives there."

"Well, check anyway," she insisted. Her fingers dug into what little muscle he possessed, sending spikes of pain through his upper arm. "I'm tired of wandering around this godforsaken country."

He nodded, said "Yes, dear," and pulled off the road into the driveway of the isolated farmstead.

The boys in the back discarded their comics, craning their necks to see where their sudden detour was taking them. "Neat-O!" said Roger. "A haunted house!"

Yes, thought Fred. That was exactly what it looked like. A house occupied only by ghosts, by the spiritual remnants of the unliving. As he parked a short distance from the building and put the Chevy in park, Fred examined it from the warmth and safety of the automobile. It was a typical example of the Midwestern farmhouse—two-storied, white clapboarded, its pitched roof and the overhang of the porch covered with a blanket of new December snow.

He regarded the windows from his vantage point. A few were boarded over or covered with sheets of curling tarpaper, while others were merely shuttered or sealed off with blinds. The narrow porch was barren. No picturesque rocking chairs or romantic hanging swing adorned it, just naked floorboards and a weathered front door with no screen.

Agnes nudged him in the ribs with a fleshy elbow. "Well, what are you waiting for? Get out and ask."

"I really don't think there's anyone here," he told her, knowing there was no use in arguing about it.

"Humor me," said Agnes in a voice that told him that she very much needed to be humored.

Fred shrugged and, opening the door, stepped into the cold afternoon air.

"Can I go with him, Mom?" asked Teddy. "I gotta pee."

"Me, too." Roger tugged on his coat, as well as his genuine Davy Crockett coonskin cap. "Real bad."

Agnes frowned, partly out of disgust and partly from an overly sour lemon drop. "Okay, go on. But you'd better do your business and do it right. This is definitely the last pit stop we're making until we get to your Uncle Ben's."

The boys piled out of the back of the car and joined their father, who was stepping through the slushy snow and making a slow trek to the front porch of the house.

"Betcha there's a ghost in there," said Teddy. "A headless man who carries around a bloody axe, looking for another noggin to replace his lost one."

Roger giggled with delight. "Naw, even better... a flesh-eating ghoul who digs up graveyards and breaks into tombs."

Fred looked around at the youngsters as they ran across the yard and hopped up on the porch. "You boys should've stayed in the car."

"We gotta pee."

"All right. There's an outhouse around back. But you boys be careful. Don't go falling into the hole."

The brothers thought that was hilarious. Their laughter rang through the rural silence like a jarring intrusion as they disappeared around the side of the house, sending clods of snow and mud flying beneath their churning feet.

Fred knocked on the top panel of the front door. The sound of his knuckles on the bare wood echoed through the old house. He stood there for a long moment, listening, hearing nothing within. He tried again, putting more force into it this time. Still no answer.

He turned back to the car. Agnes scowled through the Chevy's windshield, motioning for him to try around back.

Fred knew he would get no peace until he did as she said, so he left the empty porch and walked around the right side of the house.

When he made it around back, he noticed that the outhouse door was open, but that there was no one inside. *Maybe they did fall in*, he told himself. But his sudden fear faded when he spotted their tracks in the snow, leading both to the privy and then back again to the rear of the old house.

"Teddy, Roger… are you in there?" He went to the screen door and found the inside door open, revealing the shadowy interior of a summer kitchen. Reluctantly, he stepped inside.

It took a moment for his eyes to adjust to the murky surroundings. The summer kitchen was nearly empty. Only a few crates and heaps of trash and old newspaper furnished the cramped room. He walked to a dark corner where a rope was slung over a ceiling beam. At the end of the rope was a crude, wooden crossbar.

Fred crouched and examined the dusty planks of the floor, directly beneath the block-and-tackle. A broad, tacky stain dyed the boards a rusty reddish-brown. Blood. Obviously, the owner of this place was a hunter and used the summer kitchen to dress out his game. The crossbar would have been strong enough to suspend a good-sized deer by its hind feet.

He stood there and stared at the contraption for a long moment. Soon, his imagination played out a grisly scene. He could see Agnes hanging from the crossbar by her heels, naked and submissive… the hunted. And he was a hunter, standing before her, long-bladed knife firmly in hand, ready to butcher her like a hog.

Fred turned his eyes from the crossbar and cleared his head of the disturbing tableau. At first, he was appalled at having

conjured such a thought. But then again, he couldn't help but
admit a lingering satisfaction. He was sure some psychiatrist
would have had an appropriate term for his gruesome, little
fantasy, or maybe some high-browed explanation about a
passive husband's underlying hatred for his domineering wife.
Not that Fred would have ever thought of actually telling a
shrink about his daydreams. In that day and time, revealing
such things about one's psyche could land you in a rubber room
in a sanitarium.

A noise from somewhere inside the house drew Fred's
attention and he stepped into the household's working kitchen.
Once again he called out "Hello, anybody home?" The rafters
creaked overhead, as if someone walked across the upstairs
floor. "Teddy? Roger? Are you boys up there?"

He received no reply.

The regular kitchen was even more cluttered than the
adjoining room. There were the usual furnishings: a cupboard,
an old iron cook stove, and a kitchen table with four straight-
back chairs. He had to climb over a heap of refuse in the floor.
Junk was everywhere: burlap bags, cardboard boxes full of
yellowed newspaper and old detective magazines, and empty
tin cans and bottles with remnants of food still clinging to the
insides. The kitchen windows were shuttered, allowing only a
few slashes of pale gray light through the wooden slats.

He was stepping over a carton of *Startling Detective* and *True
Crime* magazines, when muffled laughter echoed from the upper
floor. His heart leapt to his throat, for he couldn't determine
whether the sound was that of a child or an adult.

Fred lost his balance and bumped against the edge of the
table. Among the clutter of empty packages and dirty dishes
was an oddly-shaped soup bowl made of hard pottery or plaster.
His agitation at the unexpected noise upset the bowl, causing it
to rock on its uneven base and spill the dregs of chicken noodle
soup on the tabletop.

He then began to notice some strange things. A couple of
books lay next to the soup bowl. One was the Holy Bible, while
the other was a volume called *Peckney's Science of Embalming.*
And the wicker upholstery of the kitchen chairs seemed to have

been refurbished with narrow strips of supple leather. He laid his hand on the interlaced seat of the chair nearest him. It was the finest example of hide tanning he had ever come across.

In fact, it was almost as soft as Agnes's skin… and nearly as repulsive to the touch.

The spell of creepiness conjured by the isolated house broke when the drumming of feet descended the staircase of the outer hallway. Teddy and Roger burst into the kitchen, giggling, their eyes bright with excitement. They grabbed their father's hands and began to drag him to the stairway. "Come with us, Dad," they urged. "You gotta see all the neat stuff that's upstairs!"

Fred didn't want to go upstairs, though. "We're trespassing here, boys," he said with as much parental authority as he could muster. "If the owner came back and found us, we'd be in a lot of trouble."

"Aw, come on, Dad! Please?"

Fred was firm. "No. Now let's get back to the car."

With moans of disappointment, the boys ran down the short hallway and through the kitchen to the back door. As Fred turned from the stairs, he found himself staring through the open door of a cramped living room. The windows were shuttered, but through the gloom, he could see the shape of a Christmas tree, a blue spruce from the looks of it. It was decorated with objects he couldn't quite make out in the shadowy chamber. Lank, bulky, pale gray, blush pink, or putrid green in color. A stench emanated from the room like a nest of dead mice… or something worse.

He considered going in and examining the tree closer, but something told him not to. Something told him to leave well enough alone.

When he got to the car, the boys were already climbing into the back seat. Agnes was waiting with a glare on her face. "Well?"

"Like I said, there was no one home." Fred started up the Chevy and began to back out of the driveway.

The boys' excitement hadn't abated since leaving the house. "You oughta have seen all the great stuff that was stashed upstairs!" piped Teddy with a grin.

"Oh, really?" asked their mother absently, more interested in lemon drops and finding something other than a "hick station" on the radio than anything the children might have to say.

"Yeah! In one bedroom there were masks made out of real human faces hanging on the walls and bleached skulls sticking on the bedposts."

"And that wasn't all!" added Roger. "In the closet there was a woman's skin hanging up like a suit of clothes, with bosoms and everything, and there was a Quaker Oats box full of noses. And in a shoebox there were a bunch of funny-looking things that kinda looked like hairy, little mouths…"

Agnes's face loomed over the edge of the front seat, beet red and furious. "All right, that's quite enough! Hand them over, right this moment!"

The boys stared at her with a mixture of innocence and fear. "Hand *what* over?"

"You know what I mean! Those blasted comic books!"

Glumly, Teddy and Roger surrendered their copies of *Tales from the Crypt* and *The Vault of Horror*. With an angry flourish, their mother snatched the EC comics from them and tossed them onto the floorboard at her feet.

"I've had enough of this garbage! I won't have my children turning into weirdos or juvenile delinquents!"

"I think you're overreacting, dear," said Fred as he steered the car back onto the road. "I grew up with monsters and ghosts when I was a kid. It's just harmless fun, that's all."

Agnes was unswayed in her opinion, however. "Frankenstein and Dracula are one thing. Mutilation, walking corpses, and cannibalism are quite another. Just like that Senate subcommittee says, these confounded horror comics are ruining our children's moral values and leading them down the road to depravity!"

There was nothing more to be said. The children sank into deep despair in the back seat, knowing that no amount of whining or pleading would return their precious comics to them. And Fred wasn't about to push the issue. If he did, Agnes would be sure to blame him for the boys' preoccupation with the macabre and begin one of her endless monologues about his many failures as a husband and father.

Silently, Fred shifted into gear and headed north down the secluded, rural road.

They had only gone a few yards when a maroon sedan—a '49 Ford from the make and model—turned a curve and headed toward them in the opposite lane.

"There's a car," said Agnes. "Wave it down and see if you can find out where we are."

Fred complied, honking his horn and waving out the side window. The Ford eased to a halt beside the Chevy and the driver rolled down his window. The man was a farmer by the looks of his clothing: denim overalls, a woolen coat, and a plaid deer hunter's cap. He was slightly built, his features average in many ways, except for a drooping left eye and a silly little grin on his stubbled face.

"Excuse me," said Fred almost apologetically. "But could you tell me how to get to Plainfield?'

The man in the car smiled sheepishly and nodded. "Sure. It's about seven miles straight ahead of you. It's kinda small, but you can't miss it."

"Thanks," replied Fred. "And Merry Christmas."

The fellow in the plaid cap nodded. "Merry Christmas to you."

Before the two drivers rolled up their respective windows against the bite of the December cold, their eyes met for an instant. They exchanged something then, something that had more to do with feelings than words spoken aloud. Fred couldn't figure out precisely what it was. Maybe a mutual understanding. Maybe a fleeting link between two kindred spirits who would meet only once during a lifetime, then move on, never to cross paths again.

And there was something else, something mildly disturbing—a sharing of dark emotions such as loneliness and utter despair. Emotions best concealed in the far reaches of the mortal mind... like refuse and filth hidden behind the shuttered windows of a desolate farmhouse.

The friendly motorist gave Fred a twisted grin and drove on. Fred did likewise. He glanced in the rearview mirror and saw the maroon automobile slow in front of the farmstead that the Barnett family had just left. Before turning into the rutted dirt drive, the car passed a weathered mailbox with the name GEIN painted on the side.

"Keep your eyes on the road, for God's sake!" snapped Agnes. "It's icy and slick! You want to kill us all before we even get there?"

"No, dear," replied Fred. There was an unusual edge to his voice that perhaps only he could hear. He regarded his wife's face thoughtfully. It was a deceptive face, one that was soft and fleshy, yet hard and full of cynicism. It was a face of uncompromising strength and scathing ridicule. A face that was the very opposite of his own.

As he turned his attention back to the isolated stretch of Wisconsin roadway, Fred wondered how it would feel to possess such a face and stare at the world through those cold and unforgiving eyes.

HEIRLOOMS

Tabby Monroe parked her Kia Soul at the bottom of the steep drive leading up to the cabin on Wisteria Ridge. It had snowed heavily the night before, but even if it hadn't, she still wouldn't have been able to have made it up in the little car. It would have taken something with more umph in it, as Papa used to say. Maybe a big pickup truck or four-wheel-drive. She had neither, so she parked the Kia, bundled up, and set out on foot.

She trudged through the ankle-deep snow, finding leverage to lift her to the high spots with sturdy underbrush and the lean trunks of the redbud trees she had played among as a child. She and her younger sister, Mable, had made the West Virginia mountains their playground back then. A sharp outcropping of granite for the bow of a pirate ship, a stand of long-leaf pines for a fairy wood, the old, twisted sycamore behind the house for acting out Bible stories. Mable as Zacchaeus in the branches, her as Jesus in the streets of Jericho.

After what seemed like an eternity of climbing—but was no more than fifteen minutes at the most—Tabby found herself at the old homestead. Her young life had been spent there, both good and bad, joyous and tragic. She had left the Ridge twenty years ago, hoping to put all that behind her—the poverty, the hardship, the lofty prejudices of the folks in town—but it had never really gone away. Those barefoot summers and frostbite winters, the hand-me-downs and free school lunches… all were as much a part of her as blood, bone, and sinew.

She stood there and stared at the cabin for a moment before gathering the nerve to approach. Hewn from sturdy hickory, chinked in between with deep red clay from the bottom land, the three-room structure had been there for nearly a hundred and fifty years. Great Grandpa Monroe and his family had lived there first, followed by Grandpappy Ezekiel and Grandma Missy, and, finally, Papa and Mama. After Papa had died of black lung at the age of fifty-three, Mama had been the sole occupant, living up there high in the sky by her lonesome, plying her craft for those who had need of it. That service, as well as her long life, had ended four days ago. She had been planted and prayed over in the Monroe family cemetery, thankfully before the snow and hard freeze set in.

Her mother, Latasha, or simply "Tosh" to those who knew her best, was a granny woman, even from the early age of twenty-nine. A mixer of herbs, roots, and mountain plants, a preparer of potions and poultices for anything that ailed you. They said she could predict futures from spit and dust, and speak to crows and jays like they were her children. And she could lay hands on a woman's body, whether she be pregnant or not, and tell if her firstborn would be boy or girl, or stillborn.

Mama Tosh had gotten the ways honestly. Her folks had been known throughout the Blue Ridge Mountains for healing and foreseeing. Her mother had been a granny before her and her daddy had been the seventh son of a seventh son who had never laid eyes on his own father... a man who could chase the thrush from a baby's mouth by blowing into it with his own breath and divine deep water wells in the driest of places.

Tabby had both loved and despised her mother, for many different reasons. The hatred mostly came about and festered because of Mable. Sweet, precocious Mable with the corn-silk hair and eyes as blue as new, store-bought calico. Mable, who died painfully and sadly of leukemia, because Mama had preferred her medicine over town medicine. If Mable had been born in the valley, rather than the high country, and to a family of better means and sensibilities, she might have had a chance. Instead, she had shriveled and faded like a summer flower in the frost of autumn on her fifteenth birthday.

Tabby mounted the high, timber steps to the porch and stood there for a moment. Papa's and Mama's cane-backed rockers were still there, as well as the stone mortars that Tosh had used to grind wild ginseng, Solomon's seal, and osha root for arthritis and gout, and rose pedal and dried elderberries for spring tonics and such.

She walked across the porch and opened the door. No locks had ever barred the entrance of the Monroe house. The climb was too daunting for shiftless thieves and, besides, there was nothing of worth for the taking. The main room of the cabin was nice and cozy, and had been since the summer Papa had gotten the coal company bonus and fixed the place up for Mama. Sturdy lumber and drywall had been driven all the way from Beckley, and the work had been done by hand by Papa and her Uncle Claude.

A sour taste bloomed in Tabby's mouth. Claude. She cast the unpleasant name from her mind. Born of Grandma Missy, but claimed by Old Scratch in his seventeenth year. A drifter and gambler, drunkard and whoremonger.

She turned her thoughts to other things. Comforting things, not those that bit to the quick. In the corner, between the western window and the big creek stone hearth, stood a Douglas fir anchored in a lard bucket. Mama Tosh had had it cut and brought up to her the day before her death. Her mother had loved Christmas and everything about that time of year. The Monroe place, though run-down and drab, had never looked that way in the month of December. Mama had always decorated the porch with wild holly and evergreen, had knitted stockings for the meager gifts they received from Saint Nick, and baked cakes and cookies from natural ingredients she had gleaned from the mountain wilderness.

And, more than anything else, she loved her Christmas tree and the decorations that graced it. Garlands of stringed popcorn and gooseberries, mistletoe and ribbons, foil stars, and snowflakes that Tabby and Mable had cut from newspaper using their mother's sewing scissors. And there had been the treasures… the special ones.

Tabby looked to the top of the big china cabinet with its Blue Willow dishes and oat box crystal. The shoebox was there, faded and worse for wear, as it had always been. She looked over at the tree, saddened by how very barren it appeared. Dragging a kitchen chair to the cabinet, Tabby stepped up and retrieved the box. She sat it on the little table next to Tosh's chair—the one cluttered with bottles and tins of homemade elixirs and salves for her mother's sickness—and brushed the dust from the lid. In Tosh's crude, fourth-grade penmanship was simply written *Heirlooms*.

She lifted the lid of her mother's treasure box. Inside were five ornaments nestled in cotton batting that had once been used for quilting. Balls of opaque glass heated by Mama Tosh's forge and blown into form by her own lips. The woman had tipped each with a silver stem sealed with candle wax, and the names of those who had died and gone on before them had been written, in tribute and love, across the surface of each.

She read off the names and cherished each... except one. Her papa Horace, sister Mable, Grandma Missy and Grandpa Ezekiel. And then there was Claude.

She picked up Papa's and examined it. The glass orb felt cool to the touch... so much so that the tips of her fingers fairly tingled with the chill. And it glowed a soft, icy blue from within, just like all the others. Except for her uncle's. Claude's ornament glowed cinder red and emanated a low heat, like a child's fever before spiking.

Tabby had asked her mother about them once, before leaving for life in the city. "What makes them glow, Mama? Foxfire? Maybe ghost fungus or Bitter Oyster mushroom?"

"None of those," she'd been told. "Something special. Something *everlasting*."

She recalled one year, during the trimming of the tree, Tabby had nearly dropped the glowing ball that bore Uncle Claude's name. "Take extra care with that one, Tab," her mother had said grimly. "You'd not be wanting to drop that one... and, heaven forbid, not in this house."

Her warning had puzzled Tabby at the time. *Could the contents be poisonous*, she had wondered.

In one ornament in particular, she couldn't have been any further from the truth... although she was unaware of it at the time.

Tabby cradled Papa's ornament in the palm of her hand for a moment, relishing the soft glow and the chill it emitted. She regarded the tree, pictured where Tosh had always hung it—at the top, just below the corn husk angel.

She was walking toward the tree, ornament outstretched, when the toe of her shoe snagged an uneven board. Tabby stumbled and cried out as the globe of glass and silver slipped from her grasp. Helplessly, she watched it turn, end over end, and shatter on the old hardwood floor.

What took place next was far beyond her expectation... or comprehension.

The instant the glass shattered, a blinding brilliance engulfed the interior of the cabin. An icy wind seemed to sweep the room, moving from floor to walls to the bare rafters overhead. Then the cold dissipated and warmth filled not only the house, but Tabby as well.

The brilliance settled and in its place stood a form. A tall, rawboned man in dingy, coal-blackened clothing, suspenders, and knee-high boots to protect his feet from the dank. He wore a metal helmet with a battery light on the front and carried a well-worn pickaxe in one calloused hand. As Tabby watched, he transformed, like a butterfly from a cocoon—handsome, healthy, dressed in a suit of clothes he could never have afforded on a miner's salary.

"Papa?" she muttered. The last time she'd laid eyes on that face had been amid ruffled linen and wildflowers as Lyle Paschal at the funeral home closed the casket lid before burial.

"Hi, baby doll," he said with that lopsided grin of his.

"What are you doing here?" she asked. Confusion gripped her as she dropped her eyes to the glass fragments on the cabin floor. "What were you doing in *there*?"

Her father's lean face changed. He frowned deeply and his bushy eyebrows converged until they became one. It was the expression he sported when he had something to say that you didn't want to hear.

"Tabby... did you know what your mama was? What she *really* was?"

An uncomfortable feeling took hold of her, for she had

wondered it herself many times before. "I knew she was a granny. A mountain healer."

Papa's eyes hurt with the truth of it. "Yes, she was those things. But she had a darker side. Your mother was a witchy woman, Tabby. A conjurer and spellcaster. A talker and walker with haints and boogeymen. True, she was a good-hearted woman, but she could be wicked as well."

"Did she... *put* you there? In the ornament?"

"That she did. Tosh was a loving wife and mother, but she was selfish in many ways. Couldn't bear to let loose sometimes... even in death. So she took my essence... my *soul*... and placed it in one of her treasures. Along with others that she loved... and hated."

That gave Tabby something else to dislike about her mother, along with what had happened to her sister. "I can't believe she'd do it... keep you from glory like that."

"Like the Good Book says, the afterlife is infinite. A thousand years is but a grain of sand in a desert." He smiled lovingly at his daughter. "But you've given me the means to move onward. To hear my Savior say, 'Well done, my good and faithful servant' and claim my reward."

And, with that, a heavenly portal seemed to open from the rafters overhead and the feathered arms of angels reached down and took hold of him. "No need for goodbyes, Tabby," he said. "We'll be together soon enough."

Tears streamed down Tabby's face as the cabin blazed with otherworldly light and he was gone.

She stood there, trembling and alone, for a long moment. Then she took the next ornament from the box. She looked at the name of the glass... a name that pierced her heart with a dull, mournful ache. She didn't drop it, like she had with her father's. She gently pitched it to the floorboards, frightened at what it would bring.

Again, the house filled with blinding blue light and then faded, revealing the form of a young woman. It was exactly as she feared... if only at first.

The apparition stood there—frail, pale, the flesh around her blue eyes dark and sunken from disease. Her nightgown—the one Mama had sown for a Christmas gift one winter—hung like pale drapes upon her ravaged body.

Tabby closed her eyes and prayed. *Please, Lord… do it for her. And for me.*

She felt a warmth, like the gentle breath of spring, upon her face and she opened her eyes. The one before her was now happy and full of vim and vigor. Her wavy blond hair hung luxuriantly to her shoulders and her face was pink and fresh and full. Her eyes sparkled like sapphires of the rarest form and beauty.

"Hello, Sis."

Mable's smile was like a rainbow. "Tabby! You're so beautiful! Not at all like that gangly, scarecrow of a tomboy I knew… all bruised knees and skinned elbows! A real, honest-to-goodness lady."

"You look wonderful, too," said Tabby. She could barely speak, choked with emotion as she was.

"Better than before, I reckon," her little sister admitted. "Thank you, Tabby. Thank you for doing this."

Tabby nodded, feeling as though she were in a dream. "No more pain, Mable?"

"No, sister. None whatsoever. No weakness, no sickness, no puking or pining away. Just *bliss.*"

"I'm glad." Tabby hated to see her go, but knew it wasn't her place to hinder. "Go on now. You've tarried long enough. Daddy's a-waiting."

Mable nodded. "I love you, sister. And, please… don't judge Mama so harshly. What she did for me… or didn't do… she thought for the best. It was all God's providence anyhow." Then she lifted her slender arms heavenward and was raptured away.

Tabby released her grandparents next. They laughed and talked a spell, just happy to be with one another for a short while. Tabby wanted nothing more than to run into her grandmother's arms and drink in the familiar scents of peppermint, baking cinnamon, and Gold Bond powder. And she would have loved to have wrestled playfully with her Grandpa as she once had and have him call her an old jackass until she was all laughed out. But they were different now… stripped of habit and tradition.

Ready to walk on golden streets together.

After they left her, hand in hand, Tabby turned to the box once again.

There was one heirloom left. *His.*

Mama Tosh's words came back to caution her. *Take extra care with that one, Tab. You'd not be wanting to drop that one... and, heaven forbid, not in this house.*

She considered placing the lid back on the shoebox and returning it to the china cabinet. But she couldn't stand the thought of him always being there. Glowing, warm and red and full of venom, in the darkness... confined by glass and silver, cardboard and cotton.

Carefully, she bundled herself against the cold once again, took the shoebox, and left the cabin. She descended the icy steps and stood on the bottom one. Beyond, the snowy yard stretched, with its islands of weathered stone and bramble, sweeping sharply to the road below. She considered fetching a shovel from the toolshed and burying the damned thing, but knew uncertainty and disaster lay in such a reckless act.

If what she had witnessed in the cabin remained true, then what she had in mind would not only rid her of the last ornament, but serve justice in a very real and lasting way.

Tabby took the glass ball from the box. Even through her gloves, she felt the heat of it ebb and flow, nearly burning her palm and fingers. She aimed at a clear spot fifteen feet away and, with a cry of release and anger, hurled it earthward.

The glass shattered and the snow turned from virgin white to the crimson of rage. No brilliant soul light this time, instead flames, violent and real, rising skyward. A moment later, the burning subsided and he stood there, looking as he had in her memories and her nightmares.

Big and broad-shouldered, taller and heavier than her daddy. Bearded and bear-like, he looked around, saw her standing there, and smiled. Front teeth gone from a honky-tonk brawl in Grantsville, but replaced by a country dentist with tabs of stainless steel. She could smell the stink of him from her place on the steps. Sweat, piss, the sour stench of hard liquor seeping from his pores.

"Claude," she said hoarsely. The name was a curse upon her lips.

"Well, hey," he said, cocking his head slightly. A silver grin burrowed through wayward whiskers. "How has my Play-Pretty been?"

It was a nickname she had loved him for when she was five years old… one she had loathed when he had taken her, by force, down by Willow Creek when she was scarcely thirteen.

"Holding my own," she told him. Her voice trembled and it shamed her to hear it. "In spite of you."

Claude laughed. "We'll see about that." He took a couple of steps toward her, then stopped. The others had stayed put in one spot. This one defied that rule. "Did your hellion of a mother tell you what she did to me? How I died and came to be on her damnable Christmas tree?"

Tabby said nothing. Just stared at him, eye to eye.

"She told you I left the homeplace, didn't she? That I took off to wander, the way I often did. If she did, she lied. She knew what I'd done to you at the creek bed. She could read a man that way. Study his face and mannerisms, know his thoughts and intentions. His desires."

"And she chased you off?"

"Hell no! She kilt me!" he declared angrily. "Came upon me in the dead of night, while I slept, half drunk, in the corn crib. Cleaved my skull in half with an axe, clear down to the neckbone. Then she and my brother—my own flesh and blood—buried me in the crab apple grove behind the barn."

"You deserved worse than that," she told him. "She should have skinned you alive and nailed you to a stump, and called down buzzards to devour you, bit by bit. She had the power to do that, too."

"But she didn't, now did she? Instead, she stole my soul—as raw and maggot-ridden as it was—and imprisoned it in glass in that damned treasure box of hers. Hanging me upon green branches year after year, sitting there in her chair on a winter's night, just a grinning and gloating." Claude leered hatefully. "Oh, how I hoped and prayed that someone would rock that tree and I'd come tumbling down. I would have latched onto her right then and there, slain her and burnt her with my rage. But it was never to be... until today."

"So, you think I did you a favor by setting you free?"

He started across the snowy yard toward her, his footsteps melting snow into steam as he went. "I'm thinking a man's soul is worthless and of no use... if he has no body to house it. So, I'll take up residence in yours. I've been inside you once... this time it'll be for good."

The distance between them grew narrow. Tabby heard her mother's voice in her head. *Stand your ground, daughter,* she told her. *Stand as firm as that sycamore out back.*

Claude seemed puzzled by her boldness. "Why ain't you running away, Play-Pretty? Ain't you scared of ol' uncle any longer?"

Just wait for it, girl. It's a-coming...

When Claude was eight feet from the cabin steps, he leaned forward to take another step... but found that he couldn't. He was rooted to the spot.

"What the hell...?" he asked with fear in his eyes.

"Exactly," said Tabby.

For Uncle Claude, it wasn't a doorway to heaven or angel's arms to lift him skyward. Instead, fiery tentacles laced with jagged hooks and spikes reached up from out of the earth and took hold of him. He thrashed and screamed as Purgatory claimed him for its own. His clothing caught fire, then his flesh and bone. It didn't take long for him to pay the price for the evil life he had led. With a burst of black fire and a cloud of ash and consumption, he was gone.

Tabby steadied herself with the stair railing. The stench of sulfur and charred flesh filled her nostrils and she fought back a rising sickness. The woman breathed the fresh mountain air in deeply, cleansing herself, putting the moment of retribution behind her.

She walked into the yard and stood over the spot where Claude had once stood. The snow had melted away and, underneath, there was only blackened grass and charred earth.

Tabby closed her eyes and smiled. "Thank you, Mama," she said softly.

When she turned back around, the cabin was there as it always had been and always would be… if she allowed it. She no longer regarded it with resentment or displeasure, but with forgiveness and new hope. It was a place she might someday bring a husband, perhaps birth and nurture babies. She might even grow feeble and old before its stone hearth, or rocking and shelling beans on the front porch with paradise yawning, vast and plentiful, before her.

And when she trimmed the Christmas tree, she would remember those who had gone before her… not with grief and regret, but with love. And the heirlooms that she cherished would reside within the treasure box of her heart, and not upon festive branches.

THE WINDS WITHIN

*I*dle hands are the devil's workshop, so goes the saying.
    Particularly in my case.

During the day, they perform the menial tasks of the normal psyche. But at night, the cold comes. It snakes its way into my head, coating my brain with ice. My mind is trapped beneath the frigid surface... screaming, demanding relief. It is then that my hands grow uninhibited and become engines of mischief and destruction.

As the hour grows late and the temperature plunges, they take on a life of their own. They move through the frosty darkness like fleshen moths drawn to a flame. Searching for warmth.

And the winds within howl.

"Dammit!" grumbled Lieutenant Ken Lowery as the departmental alarm went off on his cell phone. He washed down a mouthful of raspberry danish with strong black coffee, then took the phone from his coat pocket and swiped the screen with his thumb, cutting the alarm short. "I knew it was going to be a pain in the ass when the department programed these alerts to go off. Makes me feel like I'm a doctor instead of a cop."

Lowery's partner, Sergeant Ed Taylor, sat across from him in the coffee shop booth, looking tanned and rested from his recent vacation to Florida. He nibbled on a chocolate-covered donut decorated with snowflake and Christmas tree sprinkles, and chased it down with hot chocolate.

"I hope it's not anything serious," said Taylor. "I don't think I could stomach bullet holes and brains my first day back on the job. Not after I've spent the last week in Disney World, rubbing elbows with Mickey Mouse and Goofy."

Lowery stared at the man with mock pity. "Oh, the tragic and unfair woes of a homicide detective."

"Okay, okay," chuckled Taylor. "Just make the call, will you?"

The police lieutenant dialed headquarters and talked to the dispatcher for a moment. When he finished, he frowned, looking more than a little pale.

"What's up? Did they give us a bad one?"

Lowery nodded. "You know that case I was telling you about earlier? The one I was assigned to while you were on vacation?"

"The mutilation murder?"

"One and the same. Except that it's *two* and the same now."

Taylor felt his veneer of tranquility melt away. The lingering effects of the Magic Kingdom faded in dreadful anticipation of blood splatter and body bags.

"Another one? Where?"

"The same apartment building," said Lowery. "Eleven forty-five Courtland Street."

"Well, I'm finished," said Taylor. He crammed the last bite of donut into his mouth. "Let's go."

"Welcome back to the real world, pal," said Lowery as they stepped into the frigid December air, climbed into their unmarked Chrysler, and headed for the south side of the city.

The apartment building on 1145 Courtland Street was one of Atlanta's older buildings, built around the turn of the century. It was unremarkable in many ways. It was five stories tall, constructed of red brick and concrete, and its lower walls were marred with four-letter graffiti and adolescent depictions of exaggerated genitalia. The one thing about the structure that did stand out was the twin fire escapes of rusty wrought-iron that zigzagged their way along the northern and southern walls from top to bottom. The outdated additions gave it the appearance of a New York tenement house, rather than anything traditionally Southern.

There were a couple of patrol cars parked out front, as well as the coroner's maroon station wagon. "Looks like the gang is all here," observed Lowery. He parked the car and the two got out.

"The dispatcher said this one was on the ground floor. The first murder was on the fourth floor. The victim was an arc-welder by the name of Joe Killian. And, believe me, it was a hell of a mess."

"I'll check out the case photos when we get back to the office," Taylor said. He followed his partner up the steps and through double doors that were decorated with a couple of holiday wreaths that had seen better days. As they entered, they passed a few curious tenants in the drab hallway. The apartment building was nothing more than a low-rent dive, a place where people down on their luck—but not enough to resort to the housing projects or homeless shelters—paid by the week to keep off of the cold winter streets. And it was unusually cold that month. It was only a few days before Christmas, but already the temperature had dipped below freezing several times.

They located the scene of the crime in one of the rear ground-floor apartments. The detectives nodded to the patrolman at the door—who looked as if he had just puked up that morning's breakfast—and then stepped into the cramped apartment. Tom Blakely from the forensic department was dusting for prints in the living room, which was furnished with only a threadbare couch, a reclining chair, and a 24-inch Magnavox.

"The ME is in the bedroom with the victim," Blakely told them, not bothering to look up from his work.

Lowery and Taylor walked into the back room. The coroner, Stuart Walsh, was standing next to the bloodstained bed, staring down at the body of the victim, while Jennifer Burke, the department's crime photographer, was snapping the shutter with no apparent emotion on her pretty face.

"Morning, gentlemen," said Walsh with a Georgia drawl. He eyed Taylor's tanned, but uneasy face. "So, how was the weather down in Orlando, Ed?"

"Warm and sunny," the sergeant said absently. He shuddered in his heavy winter coat. "Why is it so damn cold in here?" Taylor could see his breath in the still air of the bedroom.

"The furnace is on the blink. The tenants claim it's been like this for a couple of weeks now."

"Who do we have here, Stu?" Lowery asked.

"The landlord of this establishment," said the medical

examiner. "Mr. Phil Jarrett. White male, fifty-seven years of age."

"Who found him?"

"According to the officer in the hallway, a resident stopped by to pay his rent early this morning. He knocked repeatedly, but got no answer, and found the door securely locked. He then went around the side of the building, stepped onto the fire escape, and peeked in the bedroom window over yonder. That's when he discovered Mr. Jarrett in his present state."

Lowery stared at the body of the middle-aged man. "Just like the other guy?"

"Yep. Exactly the same. The same organs were taken after the throat was slashed from ear to ear, just like Killian."

"Organs?" asked Taylor.

The coroner bent down and, with a rubber-gloved hand, showed the detective the extent of the damage. "Pretty nasty, huh?"

"I'll say," said Taylor. He turned away for a moment. He always felt nauseous at the sight of mutilation, even though he had been on homicide detail for nearly ten years. "Why would someone do something like that?"

Walsh shrugged. "I reckon that's what we're here to find out." The coroner turned to Lieutenant Lowery. "Did you ever find any leads after the Killian body was found?"

"Nope," said the detective. "I haven't had much of a chance. The Killian murder was only last Friday, you know. I interviewed the landlord here. He didn't have anything useful to say. Looks like that's still the case."

Ed Taylor regained his composure and studied the body again. It was clad only in a V-necked undershirt and a pair of Fruit of the Loom boxer shorts, both saturated with gore. He stared at the ugly wounds, then glanced at his partner. "Did you interview any of the tenants, Ken?"

"Not yet," said Lowery. "But that would be the best place to start." The detective looked over at the lady photographer, who had finished taking the crime-scene photos. "Could you have some prints for us later today, Jenny?"

"I'll have some glossy eight-by-tens on your desk by noon," she promised, then glanced around the grungy bedroom with disgust. "This guy was one sick son of a bitch. Look at what he put on his walls."

The detectives had been so interested in Jarrett's corpse that they had neglected to notice the obscene collage that papered the walls of the landlord's bedroom. Pictures from hundreds of hardcore magazines had been clipped and pasted to the sheetrock. A collection of big-breasted and spread-eagled women of all sizes and races graced the walls from floor to ceiling, as well as a number of young boys and girls who were far under the legal age.

"Yeah," agreed Lowery. He spotted a naked child that bore an uncomfortable resemblance to his own six-year-old daughter. "Looks like the bastard deserved what he got. Kind of makes it a shame to book this jerk's killer. We ought to pin a freaking medal on their chest instead."

"We've got to find the guilty party first," said Taylor. "And we're not going to do that standing around here chewing the fat."

"Then let's get to work." Lieutenant Lowery clapped Walsh on the shoulder. "Send us your report when you get through with the postmortem, okay, Doc?"

"Will do," said the coroner. "And good luck with the investigation."

"Thanks." Taylor glanced at the mutilated body of Phil Jarrett and shook his head. "Hell of a contrast to Snow White and the Seven Dwarfs."

"Like I said before," Lowery told him, "welcome home."

"Pardon me, ma'am, but we'd like to ask you a few questions concerning your former landlord, Mr. Jarrett." Lowery flipped open his wallet and displayed his shield.

The occupant of Apartment 2-B glared at them through the crack of the door for a moment, eyeing them with a mixture of suspicion and contempt. Then the door slammed, followed by the rattle of a security chain being disengaged. "Come on in," said the woman. "But let's hurry this up, okay? I've gotta be at work in fifteen minutes."

Lowery and Taylor stepped inside, first studying the tenant,

Melba Cox, and then her apartment. The woman herself was husky and butch in appearance, sporting a crewcut and a high fade on the sides and back, and a hard definition to her muscles that hinted of regular weight training. The furnishings of her apartment reflected her masculine frame of mind. There was no sign of femininity in the décor. An imitation leather couch and chairs sat around the front room, and the walls were covered with Harley-Davidson posters. The coffee table was littered with stray cigarette butts, empty beer cans, and militant feminist literature.

"Really nothing much to say about the guy, is there?" asked the woman. "He's dead, ain't he?"

"Yes, ma'am," said Taylor. "We just wanted to know if you have any idea who would kill Mr. Jarrett? Did he have any enemies?"

"Oh, he had plenty of enemies," declared Cox. "Me included. Jarrett was a real prick. Always hiking the rent, never fixing a damn thing around here, and always making lewd remarks to the women in the building. He tried to put the make on me once. I just about castrated the asshole with a swift kick south of the belt buckle."

"What about the other victim? Killian?"

Melba Cox frowned. "Didn't know him very well, but he was a sexist pig, just like Jarrett was. Just like all men are."

"Have you seen or heard anything out of the ordinary lately?" Taylor asked. "Arguments between Jarrett and a tenant, maybe? Any suspicious characters hanging around the building?"

"Nope. I try to keep my nose out of other people's business, and hope that they'll do the same." She glanced at a Budweiser clock that hung over the sofa, then scowled at the two detectives. "I gotta go now. Unless the Atlanta PD wants to reimburse me for docked pay, that is."

"We've got to be going ourselves," said Lowery as they stepped into the hallway. He handed her one of his cards. "We would appreciate it if you would give us a call if you happen to think of anything else that might help us."

Melba Cox glared at the card for a second, then stuffed it

into the hip pocket of her jeans. "Don't hold your breath," she grumbled, then headed down the stairs, dressed in an insulated jacket and heavy, steel-toed work boots, and toting a large metal lunchbox.

"Wonderful woman," said Taylor.

"Yeah," replied Lowery. "She'd make a great den mother for the Hell's Angels." His lean face turned thoughtful. "She might just be the kind who would hold a grudge against a guy like Jarrett, too. And maybe even do something about it."

"Won't you gentlemen come in?" asked Dwight Rollins, the tenant of Apartment 3-D. "Don't mind old Conrad there. He won't bite you."

Lowery and Taylor looked at each other, then entered the third-floor apartment. The first thing that struck them about Rollins was that he was blind. The elderly, silver-haired man was dressed casually in slacks and a wool sweater, giving him the appearance of a retired college professor. But the effect was altered by the black-lensed glasses and white cane. The dog that lay on the floor was the typical seeing-eye dog—a black and tan German Shepard.

"We didn't mean to disturb you, Mr. Rollins," said Lowery, "but we wanted to ask you a few questions concerning the recent deaths of Phil Jarrett and Joe Killian."

Rollins felt his way across the room and sat in an armchair next to a little Christmas tree on an end table. The artificial tree was missing a few branches and was haphazardly decorated with time-worn ornaments. "Terrible thing that happened to those fellows, just terrible. Not that I'm surprised. This certainly isn't one of Atlanta's most crime-free neighborhoods, you know. Some young hoodlum broke into my bedroom six months ago. The bastard slugged me with a blackjack while I was asleep and stole my tape player and all my audiobooks. Now why would someone stoop so low as to steal from a blind man?"

"There are a lot of bad apples out there, sir," said Taylor. "Some would mug their own grandmother for a hit of crack. About Jarrett and Killian...what sort of impression did you have of them?"

"Killian was nice enough. He was a welder. I could tell that by the smell of scorched metal that hung around him all the time. I never said much to the gentleman, though. Just an occasional 'hello' in the hallway." The old man frowned sourly at the thought of his landlord. "Jarrett was a hard man to deal with sometimes. He could be downright dishonest. He tried to cheat me out of rent money several times, telling me that a ten was a five, or a twenty was a ten. I'd never let him hornswoggle me, though. The bank where I cash my disability checks always Braille mark the bills for me. Of course, I really couldn't say much about Jarrett's treachery. A blind man has a hard enough time making it on his own, without making an enemy of the one who provides a roof over his head."

"Have you seen—" Embarrassed, Lowery corrected himself. "Have you *heard* anything out of the ordinary lately? Strangers? Maybe an argument between Jarrett and one of the other tenants?"

"There's always some bad blood in a place like this, but nothing any worse than usual." The old man's face grew somber. "I have had the feeling that somebody's been prowling around the building, though. I've heard strange footsteps in the hallway outside. Several times I've felt like someone was standing on the other side of my door, just staring at it, as if trying to see me through the wood." He reached down to where he knew the dog lay and scratched the animal behind the ears. "You've sensed it, too, haven't you, Conrad?"

The German Shepard answered with a nervous whine and rested his head on his paws.

"Well, we won't keep you any longer, Mr. Rollins," said Taylor. He caught himself before he could hand the man one of his cards, giving Rollins the number vocally instead. "Please give us a call if you think of anything else that could help."

"I surely will," said Dwight Rollins. "Do you think the murderer lives here in the building?"

"We can't say for sure, sir. It's a possibility, though."

"Lord, what's this world coming to?" muttered Rollins. "Well, at least I've got good locks on my door. Somebody would have to be a hell of a Houdini to get past three deadbolts."

The two detectives said nothing in reply. They thought it best not to upset the old man by telling him that, strangely enough, the apartment doors of both Jarrett and Killian had been securely locked from the inside, both before and after the times of their murders.

"Who the hell is it?" growled a sleepy voice from Apartment 4-A.

"Atlanta Police Department, sir," called Lowery through the door. "We were wondering if we could talk to you for a few minutes?"

"Is this important?" asked the tenant, Mike Porter. "If you're selling tickets to the freaking policeman's ball, I'm gonna be mighty pissed off!"

"There's been another murder in the building, Mr. Porter," said Taylor. "We'd like to talk to you about it."

The click of deadbolts and the rattle of chains sounded from the other side, then the door opened. A muscular fellow with dirty blond hair and an ugly scar down one side of his face peered out at them. "Somebody else got fragged?" he asked groggily. "Who was it this time?"

"The landlord," said Lowery. "Mr. Jarrett."

"Well, I'll be damned," grunted Porter. He yawned and motioned for them to come inside. "You fellas will have to excuse me, but I work the graveyard shift. I catch my shut-eye in the daytime."

"We just need to know a few things. Like your impression of the two victims and if you've noticed anything peculiar around the building lately."

"Well, old Jarrett was a first-class asshole. That's about all I can tell you about him. The other fella, Killian, was an okay guy. Had a few beers and swapped a few war stories with the man. He was a die-hard Marine, just like yours truly."

Taylor walked over to a bulletin board that hung on the wall between the living room and the kitchenette. A number of items were pinned to the cork surface: a couple of Purple Hearts, an infantry insignia patch, and a few faded photos of combat soldiers in desert gear. "You were in Iraq?" he asked.

"Afghanistan," Porter said proudly. He shuffled to the refrigerator and took a Miller tall-boy from a lower shelf. "From 2008 through 2012, when things were starting to get really ugly over there." He plopped down on a puke-green couch and popped the top on his beer can.

"What about things here in the building?" asked Lowery. "Any fights or arguments between the tenants or with the landlord? Maybe someone hanging around that you didn't recognize?"

"It hasn't been any crazier than usual. I'm not surprised that it's happening, what with all the smack dealers and gangs in this part of town." Porter grinned broadly. "They just better not screw around with old Sergeant Rock here." He stuck his hand between the cushions of the couch and withdrew a Ka-Bar combat knife. "If they do, I'll gut 'em from gullet to crotch."

The two detectives left their number and exited the apartment. As they headed up the stairs to the fifth floor, Taylor turned to his partner. "Did you notice anything strange back there in Porter's apartment?"

"Other than that wicked knife and the crazy look in the grunt's eyes?" replied Lowery. "Not really. Did you?"

Taylor nodded. "Those pictures on the bulletin board. One of them showed Porter wearing something other than his dog tags."

"And what was that?"

"A necklace...made out of human ears."

"Interesting," said Lowery, recalling the mutilation of the two victims. "Very interesting."

"What do y'all want?" glared the tenant of Apartment 5-C. The skinny, tattooed redhead balanced a squalling baby on her hip as she stared at the two detectives standing in the hallway.

"We'd like to talk to you about the recent murders here in the building, ma'am," Lowery said. "May we come in for a moment?"

"Yeah, I guess so," she said. "Just watch that you don't go stepping on a young'un."

Lowery and Taylor walked in and were surprised to see

four other kids, ranging from eighteen months to five years old, playing on the dirty carpeting of the living room floor.

When they asked Florence Armstrong about the landlord, she scowled in contempt. "Jarrett got just what he deserved, if you ask me. He was white trash, that's what he was. Wasn't about to take responsibility for things that were rightly his own."

"Pardon me?" asked Taylor, trying to clarify what she was talking about.

"The one beside the TV there—the little knob-headed bastard—that's his. I came up short on the rent a couple of summers ago and Jarrett took it out in trade. Tried to get him to wear a rubber, but he was all liquored up and horny."

Lowery's face reddened slightly in embarrassment. "Uh, no need to go into your personal life, ma'am. All we need to know is if you've noticed anything strange going on in the building lately. Strangers in the hallway, or arguments you might have happened to overhear."

"Lordy Mercy!" exclaimed the woman. "If I was to pay attention to every bit of trouble that's gone on in this building, I would've gone plumb crazy by now. Half the people in this place are junkies and drunks, and the other half are losers and lunatics. You'd just as well take your pick of the litter. Anybody in this here building could've killed both those men."

"Including yourself?" asked Taylor.

"Don't you go accusing me!" warned Florence Armstrong, shaking a bony finger in his face. "True, I've been wronged more than most. But I'm too damned busy trying to put food in my babies' mouths to go getting even with every man who treated me badly. I just take my lumps and hope they don't come knocking on my door again."

After the two detectives left, they lingered outside the door, listening to the woman scream at her unruly kids.

"Notice her arms?"

Taylor nodded. "Prison tats. Women's detention. Probably Fulton or Irwin County."

"Who knows? She could be pretty handy with a shiv," said Lowery.

They called on the rest of the tenants who were there at that time of day, then headed back downstairs. It was nearly twelve-thirty when they climbed into their car and headed for a rib joint on Peachtree Street. "So, what do you think?" asked Taylor. "Do we have a suspect somewhere in that bunch?"

"Maybe," said Lowery. "Or our killer might be a neighborhood boy. A pusher or a pimp that Jarrett and Killian might have wronged in the past."

"Or we could have something a little more sinister on our hands. Maybe a serial killer. That's just what we need...a manhunt and mandatory overtime right around Christmas time."

"Let's not go jumping to conclusions just yet," Lowery told his partner.

"This is just a couple of murders in a sleazy apartment building in South Atlanta, not some Thomas Harris novel. We'll grab a bite to eat, then head back to the office and check out the crime-scene photos and Walsh's autopsy report. Later this evening we'll go back and interview the tenants we missed the first time around."

"Sounds good to me," said Taylor. "I just hope we come up with something concrete pretty soon. I have a bad feeling that this could turn into a full-scale slaughter before it's over and done with."

"Yeah," agreed Lowery. "I'm afraid you might be right about that."

The warmth has gone and the chill of the winter twilight invades me once again, freezing the madness into my brain. My hands shudder and shake. They clench and unclench, yearning for the spurt of hot blood and the soft pliancy of moist tissue between their fingertips. The damnable winds must be stopped! They must be driven away. And only death can provide that blessed relief.

But I must be careful. The first was easy enough, and so was the second, but only because no one expected it to happen again so soon. The next time might very well be the last. But it simply must be done.

There is no denying that. Even if there are suspicious eyes and alert ears on guard throughout the building, I must let my hands do the work that they are so adept at. I must allow them to hunt out the warmth necessary to unthaw my frozen sanity.

Oh, that infernal howling! The howling of those cold and icy winds!

Lowery and Taylor were going over the coroner's report and the 8x10s of the two victims, when a call came in from Doctor Walsh. Lowery answered and listened to the medical examiner for a moment. Then he hung up the phone and grabbed his coat from the back of the chair. "Do you still have those binoculars in your desk drawer, Ed?" he asked hurriedly.

Taylor recognized the gleam of excitement in his partner's eyes. "Sure," he said. "What's up? Did Walsh come up with something important?"

"Yep. He found some incriminating evidence on both of the bodies."

"What did he find?" pressed Taylor. He retrieved the binoculars from his desk and grabbed his own coat.

"I'll fill you in on the way," said Lowery with a grim smile. "Let's just say that I think our killer is going to strike again, sooner than we think. And I have a pretty good idea who it is."

The blanketed form was so sound asleep that it didn't hear the metallic taps of light footsteps on the fire escape. Neither did it hear the rasp of the bedroom window sliding upward, giving entrance to a dark figure with the glint of honed steel in hand.

The snoring tenant knew nothing of the intruder, until she felt the weight of the body pressing on her chest and the edge of a knife blade against the column of her throat. She lay perfectly still, afraid to move, waiting for the fatal slash to come. But the action was delayed. Instead, she felt a hand creep along her flesh, the fingers clenching and unclenching, searching through the darkness. Suddenly, she recalled the rumors that had been going around the building that day. Rumors of the organs that had been forcefully taken from Phil Jarrett and Joe Killian.

Then, abruptly, the room was full of noise and commotion. She heard footsteps coming from the direction of the open window, as well as the sound of cursing. Abruptly, the weight of her attacker was pulled off of her, along with the sharpness of the deadly blade.

Melba Cox reached over and turned on the lamp beside her bed.

The two detectives who had visited her earlier that morning were standing in the room. The one named Taylor was beside the window, holding a 9mm pistol in his hand. The other, Lowery, was pressing the attacker face-first down on the hardwood boards of the bedroom floor. As Melba climbed shakily out of bed, she watched as the detective cuffed the killer's hands.

"Are you alright, ma'am?" asked Taylor, holstering his gun and walking over to her. She saw that he had a pair of binoculars hanging around his neck.

"I think so," she muttered. She pressed a hand to her throat, but found no blood there.

Then the face of the sobbing intruder twisted into view and the woman got a glimpse of who her assailant had been. "You!" she gasped. "I would've never figured you to be the one!"

The wail of sirens echoed from uptown, heading swiftly along Courtland Street. A frigid winter wind whistled through the iron railing of the fire escape and whipped through the open window. The blustery chill caused Melba Cox and the two policemen to shiver, but it made the captured murderer howl in intense agony, as if the icy breeze were cutting past flesh and bone, and flaying the tortured soul underneath.

It was two o'clock in the morning when Ken Lowery and Ed Taylor stood in the main hallway of their precinct, drinking hot coffee in silence. They dreaded the thought of entering the interrogation room and confronting the murderer and mutilator of Jarrett and Killian. The suspect had stopped their cries of torment when brought into the warmth of the police station. That was probably what had spooked the homicide detectives the most. Those awful screams blaming the winter winds on the madness that had taken the lives of two human beings.

"Well, I guess we'd better get it over with," said Lowery, draining his Styrofoam cup and tossing it into a wastebasket.

"I reckon so," said Taylor. He thought of the suspect and shuddered. He secretly wished he had taken two weeks of his vacation time instead of only one. Then he would have been fast asleep in an Orlando hotel room, rather than confronting a psychopath in the early hours of the morning.

They opened the door and stepped inside. The suspect was sitting at a barren table at the center of the room. Fingers that had once performed horrible mutilation by brute strength alone now rested peacefully on the table's surface. There was an expression of calm on the suspect's face. The cold December winds had been sealed away by the insulated walls of the police station, returning the killer to a sense of serenity. It was a serenity that was oddly frightening in comparison to the tormented screams that had filled the car during the brief ride back to the precinct.

"You can go now, Officer," Taylor told the patrolman who had been keeping an eye on the suspect.

"Thanks," said the cop, looking relieved. "This one really gives me the creeps."

After the officer had left, Lieutenant Lowery and Sergeant Taylor took seats on the opposite side of the table and quietly stared at the suspect for a moment.

"What put you onto me?" the killer asked. "How did I slip up?"

"The coroner found some strange hair samples on the bodies of Jarrett and Killian," Lowery told him. "Dog hair. And you were the only one in the building who was allowed to keep an animal."

Dwight Rollins smiled and nodded. "Unknowingly betrayed by my best friend," he said, then bent down and patted the German Shepard on the head. "I don't blame you, though, Conrad. I should have brushed off my clothes before I went out."

The dog whimpered and licked at its master's shoes. Lowery and Taylor had brought the dog along, hoping that it would pacify the old man. But only the warmth of the interrogation room had quelled the imaginary storm that raged in the blind man's mind.

"Can we ask why, Mr. Rollins?" questioned Lowery. "Why did you do such a terrible thing?"

Rollins calmly reached up and removed his dark glasses. *"This* is why."

"Good Lord," gasped Taylor, grimacing at the sight of the man's eyeless sockets.

"It happened when I was a child," explained Rollins. "I was running like youngsters do, not really watching where I was going. I tripped and fell face-down into a rake that was buried in the autumn leaves. The tines skewered both my eyes and blinded me for life. I used to have glass eyes, you know, during happier and more prosperous days. But hard times fell upon me and I had to pawn them to buy groceries. I had no idea what a horrible mistake that was."

"And why was that?" asked Lowery. He tried to lower his gaze, but the gaping black pits in the man's face commanded his attention, filling him with a morbid fascination.

"I could have never foreseen the horror of the winds," he said. "They've tormented me during these first days of winter. They squeezed past my glasses and swirled through my empty eye sockets, turning them into cold caves. And do you know what lurked in the damp darkness of those caves, gentlemen? Demons. Winter demons that encased my brain in ice and drove me toward insanity. I would have become a raving lunatic, if it hadn't been for my hands." He brought his wrinkled hands to his lips and kissed them tenderly. "They saved me. They found the means to seal away the winds...if only for a short time."

Taylor felt goosebumps prickle the flesh of his arms. "You mean the stolen organs? The eyes of Jarrett and Killian?"

"Yes. They blocked out the winds. But they didn't last for very long. They would soon lose their warmth and feel like cold jelly in my head." A mischievous grin crossed Rollins's cadaverous face, giving him the unnerving appearance of a leering skull. "You know, I was wearing them when you gentlemen came to call."

"Wearing them?" asked Lowery with unease. "You don't mean—"

"Yes," replied Rollins. "Jarrett's eyes. I was wearing them when you came to my apartment yesterday morning." The old man put his glasses back on. "And you didn't even know it."

An awkward silence hung in the room for a moment, then Taylor spoke. "You'll be transferred to the psychiatric ward of the city jail across town. A couple of officers will take you there later this morning. You'll remain in custody until your arraignment, after which you'll likely be sent to the state mental hospital. There you'll be evaluated to see if you're psychologically fit to stand trial."

"Very well," said Rollins passively. "But I do hope that the cell they put me in is well heated."

"We'll make sure that it is," promised Lieutenant Lowery. "I'm afraid that you won't be able to take your dog with you, though. It's against departmental policy, even given your handicap. But we'll see to it that Conrad gets a good home. Maybe we can find some blind child who needs a trained guide dog."

"That would be nice," said Rollins. "But couldn't he just ride to the jail with me? That wouldn't hurt, would it?"

"No," allowed Lowery. "I suppose we could bend the rules just this once."

"God bless you," said the old man. He leaned down and hugged his dog lovingly.

After calling for an officer to watch the confessed murderer and leaving instructions for those who would transport Rollins to the main jail, Ken Lowery and Ed Taylor left the station, hoping to get a few hours' sleep that morning. As they walked through the precinct parking lot, a stiff winter breeze engulfed them, ruffling their clothing and making them squint against the blast of icy air.

Before reaching their cars, each man put himself in the shoes of Dwight Rollins. They wondered how they might have reacted if the cold winds had swirled inside their own heads, and if they might not have grown just as mad as the elderly blind man under the same circumstances.

It is cold here in the police van. The officers who are driving me to my incarceration claim that the heater is broken and tell me to quit complaining, so I do. I sit here silently, enduring the creeping pangs of winter, hoping that I can make it to the jailhouse before a fine blanket of frost infects the convolutions of my aged brain and once again drives me toward madness.

A mile. Two miles. How far away is the comforting warmth of my *designated cell? It is dark here in the back of the van. Dark and as cold as a tomb. My hands jitter, rattling the handcuffs around my wrists. I try to restrain them as they resume their wandering. Through the shadows they search for the warmth that I must have.*

My friend. My dearest friend in the world...I am so very sorry. But it shall be over soon enough, I promise you that. You must remain faithful, my dear Conrad. You must serve me in death, just as you have in life.

You must help me block out the winds. Those horrible winds within.

THEN CAME A WOODSMAN

The woodsman's axe cut deep.

Up and over his shoulder, in broad, heavy strokes, it whistled through the crisp winter air. It struck again and again, its head gleaming like pure silver. It would have taken an ordinary man several dozen blows to have chopped down such a tree. But the woodsman, with his skill and strength, dropped the mighty oak with only eight.

With a splintering crack, the trunk gave way and it came crashing earthward into deep drifts of virgin snow. He heard a grumble from the neighboring trees, but ignored them. Standing abreast of the oak, he finished the job, cleaving away branches for kindling, then separating the trunk into quarters.

When he was finished, he rested. He set his axe aside and sat with his back to a large boulder. He was not exhausted, not even the least bit tired…such was his nature. But he rested nonetheless, before continuing to the next stand of trees.

As he sat there, he listened to the sounds of the forest. Cardinals sang in the barren treetops, while a black crow cawed boldly from a thicket of holly near the road. They rang like a symphony in his ears, but he derived no enjoyment from it. He felt little pleasure from such simple things, or even the fact that it was Christmas once again…although he once had with much anticipation and delight.

The crunch of footsteps came from the direction of the snowy pathway that wound through the deep forest. They were light and carefree, skipping along happily. He turned his head to see a young girl dressed in a red cloak and hood. She toted a wicker basket of Christmas goodies in the crook of one arm.

From the depths of the basket he could smell the pleasant aroma of spiced wassail, freshly-baked tea cakes, and gooseberry jam. The woodsman's stomach was empty, yet he felt no hunger.

He considered calling out to her, perhaps even to wish her Season's Greetings, but refrained from doing so. He didn't want to frighten the child.

Then she was gone on her merry way. The woodsman sat there, remembering a similar child—also a girl—from another time and place. It pained him to think of her, as well as the others. Soon, his thoughts grew heavy, much heavier than the axe he had wielded all morning, and, despite the December chill, he soon fell into a light, yet troubled, slumber.

He had once been a happy man—a man of the forest who seemed to be a very part it, both in body and soul. He was thoroughly in tune with nature. Since his boyhood, he had roamed the dense woods, had known every pine grove and canebrake, every rabbit hole and beehive. As a young lad it wasn't uncommon to find him running with the deer, swimming with the fish in the lake north of the big bright city, or wrestling with snakes in the green moss beds.

Later, as a man who had taken on the apprenticeship of a woodcutter, his family made his life even more complete. His wife was a lovely, sensible woman from the village and his children—a boy and a girl—were his pride and joy. It was a pleasure to return to his cottage following a hard day's work to find a bountiful meal on the table and cheerful greetings as he walked through the door. Later, after supper, he would take his pipe and retire to the bench before the hearth. His little ones would sit at his knees, eager to hear about that day's labor and what strange animals he had encountered.

Then came that fateful night ten years ago, when the woodsman's life had changed forever.

He had tackled a particularly stubborn stand of timber that day and had lost track of time. As the last tree fell, dusk was giving way to twilight. He set off down the cobbled pathway, aware that it was long past his suppertime. He was certain to receive a sound scolding from his wife for being so late.

As he traveled the dark forest, he became aware that something was wrong. The woods were too quiet. Nary a cricket or toad sang, nor did he hear the lonesome call of the nightbird. There was only a thick and oppressive silence, as though the wildlife of the forest had been startled into a frightened hush.

He quickened his pace. Somewhere ahead came the howl of a wolf—not a long, mournful call, but one that was savage and strangely triumphant. He looked skyward. Above the treetops hung a full moon. It was a pale red in color...a blood moon, as the old tales called it. A bad omen that heralded heartache and disaster.

Soon, he was running toward the low, thatched structure of his home. Before long, he saw it ahead in a clearing, but it held none of the inviting warmth it normally did. No smoke drifted from the stone chimney and no lamplight shown from the windows.

The place was dark and desolate...like a tomb.

When he reached the entrance, he found that the door had been ripped from its iron hinges by brutal force. The oaken boards were deeply scored, as if by the claws of some horrid beast.

As he prepared to enter the house, a cloudbank drifted in front of the moon, casting a blanket of gloom over the forest. He heard movement within the black pit of the doorway, as well as a low, guttural breathing. His heart pounded in his chest as he gripped the axe handle firmly and cautiously stepped inside.

"Rebecca?" he called out. "Children?"

For a long moment, complete darkness occupied the cottage. Then the cloudbank moved onward and moonlight shown through the windowpanes, revealing the horror that stood before him.

It was a wolf, or something much worse than one. It was tall and brawny, its coarse gray fur glistening like spun silver in the light of the full moon. It crouched in the center of the cottage's main room, tearing at something with its massive fangs. Then, slowly, it rose, standing on its hind legs like a man. The tips of the wolf's ears touched the oaken beams of the ceiling, which were located a good eight feet from the floorboards.

In the pale glow, the woodsman took in the carnage that had been wrought upon his home. His daughter laid limply across the eating table, amid shattered dishes. His son curled, crumpled and lifeless, on the forestone of the hearth, his head twisted and at odds with the rest of his body. The thick stench of fresh blood hung heavily in the air, the same way the heady scent of honeysuckle and pine fills the air of the forest.

The woodsman took a threatening step forward. The beast stood there, holding the slack form of his wife. Her clothing had been partially torn away and her throat was an ugly gaping hole. The wolf bared its bloody fangs and grinned, then threw back its massive head and laughed. Laughed much in the same way a man might.

"No!" screamed the woodsman. He lunged forward, raising his axe for the swing.

But he was not quick enough. Before he knew it, the wolf had flung the woman aside and was leaping toward a side window. It crashed through the opening, taking sash, hand-sewn curtains, and glass with it.

The woodsman pursued it into the dark undergrowth. He caught a glimpse of the beast as it sprang though the trees, attempting to escape. As he set off after the fiend, he found that the forest he had grown to love was now his worst enemy. Tree limbs tore at his face and clothing, and the leafy vines of the forest floor clung to his boots, threatening to trip and drag him down.

For miles, he followed the wolf's trail, catching only fleeting glimpses of him as dark pools of shadow gave way to moonlight. The earth began to rise from the hollow of the valley. Soon, he found himself climbing the rolling green hills that stretched to the south. Exhausted, the woodsman fought the terrain, intent on making the monster pay for the atrocity it had committed. He would find the beast and kill it, or die trying.

Finally, he found that he was gaining on the beast. He paused to catch his breath and saw the wolf, crouching on a moss-covered deadfall, staring back at him. It's horrid form—half-human, half-canine—was etched against the broad pink sphere of the blood moon.

It motioned to him with long, clawed fingers. "Come, mortal!" it rasped tauntingly. "Catch me if you dare!" Then it sprang across the fallen log and vanished from sight.

With a yell, the woodman ran forward, axe raised. He leapt across the deadfall unheedingly...and found himself flailing through open air.

He discarded the axe and attempted to find something to correct his mistake. He could find no handhold, however. Like a stone, he seemed to fall endlessly. An instant later, he reached the floor of a deep canyon. He caught a flash of sharp shale and granite boulders rushing up to meet him. Then he lost consciousness with the terrible impact.

How long he laid there, he had no idea. He awoke once, in dewy darkness, wracked in agony. He could scarcely move. With incredible effort, he managed to turn his head a few inches. In the moonlight he saw shards of jagged bone jutting from his arms and legs like the quills of a porcupine. It was certain that every bone in his body had been shattered, and that he had broken both his neck and spine. When the pain grew too intense to bear, his mind served him mercifully, dragging him back into numb darkness once again.

When he awoke again it was daylight. He heard something nearby—the squeak of wagon wheels and the clatter of horse hooves on stone. Then, suddenly, he was staring into the face of a huge giant of a man with a bushy white beard and piercing green eyes. He recognized the man from the trips he had made to the village. Some called him a craftsman, some a magician.

The man crouched and studied him thoughtfully. "Yes," he said, gently lifting his broken body in his arms and carrying him to the bed of his wagon. "I shall fix you."
And so he had.

The woodsman awoke with a start. Nearly overcome with emotion, he rose to his feet.

No tears, he told himself. *You know what that gets you.*

Even after those many years, the night of the blood moon still haunted him. The horrible massacre of his family had taken away his heart. He felt hollow inside.

He discovered that his slumber had been a lengthy one. Night had fallen and only a broad, pale moon overhead gave light to the winter landscape. He picked up his axe and stepped through the snow, onto the pathway, intending to return to his labor. He was not a man to shun work, whether it be dawn or dusk. But something caused him to take pause.

It was the voice of a child.

"Oh, Grandmother, what large ears you have!" she said.

She was answered, deeply and gruffly. "The better to *hear* you with."

The woodsman started down the pathway. There was something disturbingly familiar about that voice.

He had only gone a short distance, when the voices came again.

"Oh, Grandmother, what great eyes you have!" The child was a girl from the sound of it.

Again that awful voice. "The better to *see* you with."

The woodsman began to run. He saw a small stone cottage up ahead and knew that it belonged to an old woman. He had seen her only a few days before, hanging festive boughs of holly and mistletoe from the windows and doors.

"Oh, Grandmother, what terribly sharp teeth you have!" the girl squealed in alarm.

If the woodsman intended to approach the house silently, his plan was futile. His footsteps pounded on the icy cobblestones of the pathway like the thunderous beating of a war drum.

A savage growl roared from within the little cottage. "The better to e*at* you with, my dear!"

The woodsman leapt over the gate of the iron fence and was to the door in a flash. A mighty blow from his axe split the thick wooden panel in half. He stepped inside and felt as though his troubled past had suddenly come back to torment him.

The little girl he had seen earlier—the one with the bright red cloak and hood—was running around a tall Christmas fir decorated with strings of popcorn, pinecone, and berries. She shrieked in fright as a lumbering form chased her. It was dressed in the flannel nightgown and frilly nightcap of an elderly woman. But the thing inside the clothing was far from a kindly grandmother. Massive paws bearing sharp talons protruded from the sleeves of the gown, while beneath the nightcap leered the hungry countenance of a giant wolf. A wolf with coarse gray hair.

The woodsman reached out as the girl sprinted around the holiday tree and pushed her protectively behind him. A mixture of horror and exhilaration filled him as he stood before the wolf in grandmother's clothing.

"At last I have found you, fiend!" he said. "I have searched for you for a long, long time."

The wolf roared and flexed its hirsute body. The gown ripped at the seams and fell away, revealing its hideous form. "Stand aside, enchanted one! Yield the way and give me my prey!"

The woodsman clenched the handle of his axe. "Never again, beast! Never again!"

And, with that, he swung his axe deftly and without error. The edge of the silver head bit into the sinewy throat of the wolf, severing its skull from its body. The monstrous head spun across the room—ears, snout, and all—and landed in the crackling fire of the hearth.

As the wolf's ghastly form dropped to its knees, the woodsman saw its stomach bulge. Alarmed, he watched as the imprint of a hand showed against the pale fur the underbelly.

"My grandmother!" cried the child. "He swallowed her!"

He watched as the bulge in the wolf's stomach receded. "Take heed, madam!" he yelled loudly. He swung his axe once again, this time putting the very tip of the edge into the wolf's hide. It opened the flesh from breastbone to crotch with a single, smooth stroke.

A moment later, he was helping the old woman out of the cramped confines of the beast's abdomen. She was frightened and trembling, but otherwise seemed to have suffered no harm.

The little girl stared up at their rescuer in awe. "Thank you, kind sir," she gasped. "Thank you for coming to our aid."

The woodsman's face gleamed as he smiled down at her. "You are more than welcome, Little Red."

They urged him to stay and share their holiday meal of

cakes and gooseberry jam, but he politely refrained. He left the house and went on his way, his step much lighter than it had been before.

Little Red ran to the window and watched through the frosty panes as he continued down the pathway. "What a strange man," she said in wonderment.

"Yes," said Grandmother, laying out the Christmas treats that her granddaughter had brought in her basket. "He is a peculiar gentleman, but a good one. He is known throughout the land for his strength of heart...although he would never admit it himself."

The girl continued to watch him. As he stepped out of the dark shadow of the trees and into a brilliant patch of moonlight, she squinted against the glare that he cast. His footsteps rapped almost musically on the golden bricks of the road that wound through the deep forest.

Together, Grandmother and Little Red sat down to Christmas tea. As they dined, they listened to the steady chopping that signaled that the woodsman had once again returned to his work.

Before their meal was done, the rattle of sleet could be heard upon the roof. Then, moments later, as a shift in the temperature changed the ice into a driving rain, the strike of the axe grew silent and they heard it no more.

AS FOR ME, MY LITTLE BRAIN

"Are you sure this is a good idea?"

Tom could tell that Carol was nervous. The mall was insanely busy on Christmas Eve. Wall-to-wall shoppers, seeking bargains and fighting to purchase that last gift before the big day tomorrow. She held Tina's tiny hand just a little too tightly…as though afraid the child might break free and drift off amid the waves of winter coats and shopping bags, like a rowboat lost at sea.

"Everything is going to be fine," he assured her. "We're just going to see Santa and then go home. No big deal."

His wife didn't seem convinced. "Tom, there's so many people. What if she gets…upset?"

"She'll be just fine. And so will you," he added as an afterthought.

"Let's see Santa," Tina said with that bright, infectious smile of hers. "Wanna see Santa."

Carol took a deep breath and nodded. "Okay, sweetie… we're going to see him right now."

The three began the long walk from one end of the mall to the other, past Build-A-Bear Workshop, Rue 21, and Barnes & Noble.

"Mommy, you're hurting my hand!" whined Tina.

"Sorry, sweetheart." Carol relaxed her grip, but only a little.

"Daddy?"

"Yes, pumpkin?" Tom was calm and relaxed…a rock. But, inside, his stomach felt like it was twisted into knots.

"Daddy, sing the song!" Tina piped happily. Her tiny blue eyes sparkled, one slightly askew of the other.

He knew which song she wanted to hear...and only that one, goofy stanza, not the entire thing. "Okay, here it goes." He began to sing. *"As for me, my little brain... Isn't very bright. Choose for me, old Santa Claus... What you think is right!"*

Tina laughed and giggled, jumping up and down in her Christmas-red Gymboree sneakers.

Tom glanced over at his wife. Carol looked on the verge of crying. He reached over and took her free hand as they walked. "Sweetheart, be brave. For her."

Carol nodded, lifted her head high, and continued onward. As they headed for Santa's Workshop and the great gold and red velvet throne of the Jolly One himself, she felt eyes upon them. Passing shoppers, the clerks at the kiosks...all held various expressions as they passed by. Surprise, pity, amusement, fascination. Like gawkers at a county fair sideshow.

Stop staring at her! her mind screamed. *Stop staring at my baby!*

Harvey sat there, waiting for the next child to approach. He beamed a great, white-bearded smile and unleashed a hearty "Ho, ho, ho!"

He appraised each child carefully. Some failed to pique his interest. Others were so appealing to his "obsession" that they were nearly unbearable to look at. He breathed deeply and tried quell his arousal. It was like seeing and smelling the warm cinnamon rolls in the window of the bakery shop in the food court. Tantalizing to the senses, tempting to the impulses, but presently out of reach.

Playing Santa at the mall was the best job Harvey had ever had. Better than the school bus driver, the camp counselor, the youth leader at the church in Texas.

Two kids took their turns. First a six-year-old boy who wanted Legos and Star Wars toys, then a seven-year-old girl who really, really, really wanted an iPhone, even though her parents thought she was too young to have one. Harvey had been waiting for that one kid—that little boy who wanted a BB gun—so he could say "You'll shoot your eye out, kid!" But, so far, he hadn't been that lucky.

Harvey, feeling restless, shifted on his throne and

ho-ho-hoed again. He tugged at the furry sleeve of his red suit, until his wristwatch was in view. Eight-thirty two. The mall closed at nine. Almost time to clock out.

One of the elves—a teenage girl with braces and short red hair, dressed in a green and gold pixie outfit—brought the next kid to meet Santa. As the child was led from her parents, up the snowy steps, to the platform, Harvey could tell that this one was a little different. She was a pretty little girl, dressed in a white insulated jacket, candy cane leggings, and red sneakers... but there was something about her that was slightly off-kilter. Her happy blue eyes seemed sharp and alert, but one seemed a half-inch higher than the other. And her head...her head wasn't quite right. The crown of her head, adorned with long blond curls and a pretty red bow, seemed smaller than the chubby, smiling face underneath it.

He had seen something like that before, but couldn't recall where. Then, as he reached out and sat her on his lap, Harvey remembered. An old black-and-white movie by Todd Browning. *Freaks*. Yeah...she was like Schlitzie the Pinhead.

"Well, hello, little cutie!" Harvey said in his best, booming Santa voice. "And what is your name?"

The girl, maybe five years of age, grinned up at him. "Tina!" She drew the word out, long and proud. *Teeeeena!*

The child shifted slightly in his ample lap, trying to find a secure spot. Comfortable for her, but maddening for him.

"And what do you want for Christmas, Tina?" he asked, forcing his mind out of the gutter and back into the role he had been hired for.

"I want a Wetsy Betsy...the kind that pees her diaper...and an Easy-Bake Oven with cake mix...and a pair of roller skates!"

Harvey threw his head back and laughed. "Ho, ho, ho! That's quite a haul, little lady! But I'll be sure to put it down on my list for tonight."

Tina clapped her hands. "Goody, goody!"

Harvey slipped his mittened hands beneath her arms, preparing to lower her to the floor once again. "Now, go on back to your mommy and daddy."

Tina refused to go, however. She grabbed fistfuls of his red velvet suit and held fast. "No! Not until you sing the song!"

"Uh, song?" he asked, trying to remain in character. "What song?"

"Jolly Ol' Saint Nicholas!"

"Well, Santa's not much of a singer—"

"Please, oh please...sing it to me! But only the last verse!"

Harvey had to think about it for a moment. He knew all the Christmas songs. He had sung them countless times to pacify and gain the trust of children, especially the smaller ones. Finally, it came to him.

He cleared his throat and sang in his best baritone. "As for me, my little brain... Isn't very bright. Choose for me, old Santa Claus... What you think is right!"

Tina clapped and cheered. "Thank you, Santa! Thank you!" She leaned forward and kissed his rosy cheek.

Harvey flushed hot, from head to toe, but not with embarrassment.

"Goodbye, Tina. Look for lots of good stuff from Santa beneath your Christmas tree in the morning!"

Excited, the little girl jumped down and was led down the steps back to her parents. Harvey watched and noticed that there was an odd expression of relief on the mother's face as they turned to leave. *Did she suspect something?* he couldn't help but wonder. *Was she afraid I was going to try something...right here out in the open?*

As they left Santa's Workshop, Carol clutched her daughter's hand, studying her with concern. "Are you alright, sweetheart? Did everything go okay with Santa?"

"Yes, Mommy! Yes!" laughed Tina. "I'm happy! So happy! Happy, happy, happy!"

Carol and Tom looked at one another. When Tina got happy, things seemed to go downhill...quickly.

"Let's get her to the car," he suggested.

Carol nodded and tightened her grip on Tina's hand. They quickened their pace, heading for the entrance where they had come in.

Then, abruptly, a Christmas shopper toting a 32-inch flat

screen in his arms loomed out of nowhere. Unable to clearly see what was ahead of him, he plowed into Carol, knocking her down. She lost her hold of her daughter's hand and landed flat on her back. Her purse slipped off her shoulder and its contents spilled across the tile floor of the galleria, objects skittering all directions.

"Oh, crap, lady…I'm sorry!" he apologized. "I wasn't watching where I was going!"

"That's okay," Tom said, annoyed. "I'll help her up."

The shopper nodded and left with the TV, an expression of regret on his face, but glad that he would be able to escape the mall before the stampede hit the exits and the parking lots in ten minutes.

"Just look at this mess!" Carol looked like she was at her breaking point.

"Don't worry. We'll get it all picked up," Tom assured her.

Carol looked over at her daughter, who stood there smiling. "Just stand right there, honey. Daddy and I will have this all cleaned up in a minute."

The two scrambled on their hands and knees, locating the objects from Carol's purse and putting them back in their proper place. When they finally seemed to have finished, Carol shook her head. "My phone isn't here. Where is it?"

Tom looked around. "There it is. Under that bench."

After Carol had retrieved her cell phone, she looked around and her face grew deathly pale. "Tom."

"What is it, dear?"

"Tom…Tina's gone."

He looked around frantically. The little blond girl in the white coat was nowhere to be seen.

"Oh God!" moaned Carol. "What if…what if she…?"

"Don't worry," he told her, attempting to stifle his own panic. "She couldn't have gotten far. We'll find her."

Carol spun in a circle, near hysteria. "But…but all the *people!*"

Her husband reached out and held both her arms, looking her squarely in the eyes. "Carol…everything's going to be fine. We'll find her."

Harvey had clocked out for the night and was crossing the parking lot to his van, still dressed in the Santa suit, when he heard a giggle echo behind him.

"Hi, Santa."

He looked around to find the little girl with the misshapen head standing behind him.

Harvey looked around. He couldn't believe his luck. There was no one else around. Just him and her.

"Oh, hi…" Harvey searched his brain for her name and found it. "…Tina."

The little girl hopped excitedly from one sneakered foot to the other, grinning.

The mall Santa looked over at his van and then back to Tina. "Guess what!"

"What?" replied Tina.

"Old Saint Nick has got a great big surprise for you," he said, casting the bait. "But it's in my van."

"I thought you had a sleigh with reindeer."

"Oh, I do, I do…but I drive the Santa Van when I come to the mall." Harvey felt his heart pound wildly in his chest. "So…that surprise. Do you want to see it?"

"The big surprise?" asked Tina.

Harvey's bearded grin broadened. "Yes…the *biggest*."

Tina extended her tiny hand. "Okay."

Harvey took it and led her toward the belly of the beast. He dug his key fob out of his Santa pants and opened the power door on the driver's side. It swung open on its tracks, revealing the dark interior.

"It's nighttime inside," observed Tina.

"Yes, but it's warm and cozy." Harvey had disconnected the interior lights for a specific reason.

Tina stood at the edge and peered in. "And there's no seats."

Harvey began to grow impatient. "Do you want to see Santa's surprise or not?"

Tina nodded. "Sure."

Together, they climbed inside. Harvey thumbed the fob.

The door closed slowly. When it shut, it was like the closing of a prison cell, only deceptively so.

It was pitch black in the back of the van. A dark curtain had been rigged behind the front seats and another across the rear hatch window. For a moment, all that could be heard was their breathing. Hers was small and anxious; his was rapid and close to hyperventilation.

"Are you ready for the surprise?" he asked her softly.

Tina said nothing in reply. She only giggled.

"What's so funny, Tina?"

More giggling…low and melodical…in the dark.

"Santa?"

"Yes?"

"Are you naughty or nice?"

Santa whiskers tickled his nose and cheeks as he leered. "Oh, I'm nice. Very, very nice. How about you?"

Tina was silent for a long moment. Then she replied. "I'm naughty, Santa. *Soooo* naughty."

Harvey felt like giggling himself. *That makes it so much easier,* justifying it in his mind, like he always did.

He reached out for her…and felt a thin line of pain travel across the palm of his hand.

"What the shit?" he croaked, rocking backward.

The giggling in the van grew louder…high-pitched… unstable.

He felt something split his left ear and travel toward the bridge of his nose. On its way, it punctured his eye, filling his skull with an explosion of agony. "Oh God!" he pleaded. "Oh God!"

But God didn't listen to the prayers of people like him.

He fumbled for the key fob he had laid on the van floor, but couldn't locate it in the dark. He flailed and punched at the blackness, hoping to strike the child, but she only laughed and dodged his blows. Something wickedly sharp jabbed him in the belly, was held at bay for a second, then continued onward through cloth, skin, and muscle. He felt it travel quickly to the side with a strength he would have never thought a five-year-old could possess. Abruptly, most of his intestines rolled forward and spilled heavily onto the van floor.

Harvey opened his mouth to scream, but the thing in her hand worked its unseen magic again, cleaving his larynx cleanly in half. His intended cry for help emerged as nothing more than a bloody, bubbling wheeze.

And Tina giggled...and giggled...and giggled.

Tom and Carol were in their car, driving slowly down one row of the parking lot to the next, when they saw something in the beams of the headlights.

"Isn't that Tina's hair bow?" Carol's voice was part hope and part dread.

It lay in the wash of the headlights like a crimson butterfly that had fallen from flight.

They stopped and got out, leaving the car to idle. As Carol reached down, hand trembling, to retrieve her daughter's bow, a noise caught her attention. She looked over to see a black van parked several spaces away, apart from the other vehicles.

A power door swung open and Tina leapt out, all energy and joy.

Her white jacket was blood red in color. Or, rather, red with blood.

"Look, Mommy!" Tina smeared the wet redness around and around with one small hand. "I'm Santa Claus!" Her other hand clutched a steak knife, dripping with gore and slivers of Harvey.

Carol began to cry. She sank to her knees and held her arms wide. "Come here, baby. Come to Mommy."

Stunned, Tom walked to the open door of the van and looked inside. Light from a nearby streetlight revealed all he needed—or wanted—to see. "Put her in the car," he called to his wife.

Carol held her daughter tightly, staring at her husband over the child's blood-splattered shoulder. "What did she—?"

"Put her in the freaking car!" he nearly screamed.

Five minutes later, they were three miles away from the mall and speeding down a ramp to the interstate. Tom and Carol sat in the front, staring straight ahead, while Tina sat in her car seat in the back, giggling and talking to herself.

Carol continued to cry. Tina Marie...her darling, little girl. The doctors had said that her condition was terminal...that her malformed brain—a third the size of a normal child's—would leave her as nothing more than an unresponsive vegetable. They had been wrong, though. She had grown to be a lively, fun-loving child...but one missing vital things. Things like kindness, compassion, and self-restraint.

The doctors had claimed that she would not live past her second birthday. There were times that Tom and Carol truly wished that they had been right.

"Why does she do these things?" sobbed Carol, burying her face in her hands. It was a question she had asked time and time again.

Tom had no answer for her. He clutched the steering wheel tightly and glanced in the rearview mirror every few seconds, looking for flashing blue lights, but there were none.

"Are we going to have to move again?" his wife asked him. "Change our names?" She thought of the others: the maid in San Diego, the teenage babysitter in Denver, the homeless man in the park in Cincinnati.

"Let's go home and have a Merry Christmas," Tom suggested. He wondered how they could possibly go through this one more time. "Afterwards, we'll decide."

Carol continued to weep bitterly. The bloody steak knife, which they had locked away in the pantry with all the other knives in the house, lay on the floor mat at her feet.

"Daddy?"

The muscles of his jaws tightened and, for just an instant, he considered flooring the gas pedal and driving head-on into the concrete support of an overpass up ahead. Ending it once and for all...for the three of them.

"Yes, pumpkin?"

"Daddy...sing the song!" said Tina. "Please, sing it for me again."

Tom didn't want to. God knew he didn't want to hear that damn song ever again.

But he did anyway...if only for her.

BENEATH THE BRANCHES

The kids wanted a live tree that Christmas, not the artificial one from the attic. There was a good reason for that request. Their father, who had been away for nine months serving his country, would be coming home for the holidays.

Kim Ballard set out that Saturday afternoon to find one, and her daughter, Jordan, and son, Danny, insisted on coming along. She wanted to believe it was because they wanted a little Christmas outing with their mom, but, in reality, she knew that they wanted to make sure that she picked the right tree. It would have to be absolutely perfect for Dad. They all knew that he deserved it, after being away for so long.

They took Nick's big Dodge Ram dually because they wanted at least a seven-footer. The first place they tried was the tree lot on Chestnut Avenue in Pikesville. Kim found the selection to be lacking. Most were under six feet and many had already lost a large percentage of their greenery. Besides, the lot owner, a cranky old fart named Elmer Gant, was wanting upwards of ninety to a hundred and twenty for a tree that would have been dead before Christmas Eve. Kim wasn't about to waste her money on something that Charlie Brown would have been ashamed to take home.

"Sometimes folks sell trees out on the highway," suggested Jordan. The fourteen-year-old was the spitting image of her mom: tall, blond, and as lean as a willow. "Maybe we can get a good one out there cheaper than in town."

Kim agreed. They left the town limits and headed south along Highway 100, toward the Cumberland River. They spotted a man with a horse trailer, selling a few trees and mistletoe that he had shot from the top of a tree with a shotgun… a safer way of harvesting the high-grown vegetation than shimmying up and risking a broken neck. But the trees were too dry and the mistletoe riddled with buckshot holes, so they continued onward.

When they reached the Cumberland River Bridge, where high cliffs rose above the rushing water below, they spotted an old pickup truck parked on the other side, with a dozen or so trees displayed next to it. "I think we're in luck," Kim told them.

Halfway across the bridge, Jordan looked over at her mother. "Uh, Mom…we're getting kind of close, aren't we?"

Kim knew what she was referring to. "Don't worry. We're not going over the line or anything. Just going to see what this man has to sell and head home."

Danny looked up from his phone and his game of Mortal Kombat. "What? Are you talking about Fear County?"

"Of course we are, goober!" Jordan snapped at him.

Her ten-year-old brother laughed. "Do you really believe all that hogwash? About it being the most evil place in the state of Tennessee?"

His sister shrugged. "Hey, better safe than sorry."

They made it to the other side of the bridge and pulled to the side of the highway, parking behind the truck—an old Ford, probably from the mid-'70s. The body of the vehicle was infected with rust and its tires were splattered and caked with clay mud as red as blood.

The three of them climbed out of the Dodge and walked over to see what he had available. "Hi," said Kim with a smile.

The man—short, dark-haired, and unshaven, dressed in faded overalls, a flannel shirt, and an ear-flap cap—nodded at them from where he leaned against the wall of the truck's bed. "Howdy."

Kim walked along the row of trees, examining each and every one. They were all lush and green and freshly cut, their branches folded and cinched together with heavy twine. "Nice," she said. She stopped before a particularly appealing one that must have been seven and a half feet. "How much?"

The man grinned, showing off rotten, tobacco-stained teeth.

There was something about his face that she didn't like, maybe the way his smile drooped downward on one side and upward on the other. Or how the pupils of his eyes seemed to be nearly as big as the irises. She could hardly tell what color they were, they were so dark.

"How does fifty sound to you?" he asked. He took a plug of tobacco from his overalls pocket and, with a greasy pocketknife, cut himself a chaw. Kim couldn't say for sure, but she could have sworn she saw the juice from the tobacco wiggle and run sluggishly up the flat of the blade before he put it away.

"I don't reckon you'd take a debit card, would you?"

The man laughed. "No, ma'am...I have no means to make a sale that way."

Kim opened her purse and took out her billfold. "I'm afraid I only have...let's see...twenty-eight dollars in cash."

The man didn't wait to haggle or bicker. "Sold!" He reached out with a grubby hand and snatched the bills from her grasp. "I'll load it in your truck for you."

As he picked up the tree and headed for the bed of the dually, Kim looked past the old Ford and saw the sign in the distance... the sign no one had the nerve to travel past. Not if they believed the old tales that had been told in Pikesville for as long as anyone could remember.

A sensation of dread gripped her and she almost said "No, wait!" But, she didn't. The tree was the nicest one they had come across all day and they wanted to get it home and decorated before they Skyped Master Sergeant Nick Ballard at 9:00 pm Central time, 5:00 am Kuwait time.

When the man had secured the tree in the bed, he started back to his truck and the little roadside lot of trees.

"Thank you!" Kim called out to him. "And Merry Christmas!"

He turned and flashed that unnerving topsy-turvy smile of his. "Yes, ma'am. Merry Chri—" A pained look crossed his face, as though he had caught himself before he could actually say the word. "Uh, have a good 'un."

They climbed into the cab of the Dodge, made a U-turn in the middle of the highway, and headed back home. As they drove off, all three couldn't help but glance in the rearview mirror at the tree vendor by the side of the road.

"He sure was a weird one!" said Danny from the back, rolling his eyes.

"It isn't nice talking about strangers like that," his mother scolded. "Remember, you're not supposed to judge a book by its cover." A chill ran down the back of her neck; whether it was from the December cold or something else, she couldn't tell. She looked over and saw that Jordan was just as spooked as she was. "But I will say one thing. If that man back there *was* a book…he'd probably be written by Stephen King."

When they got home, they carried the big tree through the patio doors because it was much too full to fit through the utility room door at the back of the house. The tree stand had already been positioned next to the fireplace. With some effort, Kim and Jordan wrestled the big pine to a vertical position, nearly losing balance several times. Then they slipped it into the collar of the stand, while Danny secured it tightly in place with the screw tabs.

The entire time they were at work, they failed to notice that their orange tabby, Sweetie-Pete, was perched on the back of the sofa, eyeing them and their new purchase suspiciously. Normally, the cat was busy expressing his curiosity during such projects, winding his way annoyingly between their legs as they worked and generally making a nuisance of himself. But he didn't this time. He simply crouched on the back of the couch and kept his green eyes glued, not on the Ballard family, but on the big tree they had brought home.

"Okay," said Kim. "Cut her loose!"

Jordan took a pair of scissors they had liberated from the kitchen utility drawer and cut the heavy twine that bound the branches together. With each snip, the lush green boughs unfolded and fell into place. When she was finished, they stepped back and admired the big pine.

"Wow!" said the teenager. "This has got to be nicest tree we've ever had."

Kim agreed. "It is beautiful."

It was much larger and fuller than it had appeared when they had bought it from the odd man with the pickup truck. It was at least eight feet tall, only a few feet short of touching the rafters of the living room's cathedral ceiling. And it was the darkest, richest shade of green they had ever seen.

"Just smell it!" said Danny.

The boy was right. The scent was stronger than most evergreens that had graced their home. It had a peculiar earthy, almost enchanting, odor that reminded Kim of ancient times and forgotten places. She had always been a fan of *The Hobbit* and *The Lord of the Rings*, so she didn't consider it strange that the aroma would conjure such images.

An inner branch seemed to shift and fall into place, causing the tree to shudder slightly.

Sweetie-Pete arched his striped back and hissed, almost defensively.

"What's wrong, boy?" asked Danny. He reached for the cat, intending to comfort him. But the feline was having no part of it. He shrugged away from his master and began to pace restlessly across the top of the couch, from one end to the other.

"What's crawled up his butt?" wondered Jordan.

Kim was puzzled, too. For the past couple of years, they'd had a difficult time keeping Sweetie-Pete away from the Christmas tree and its ornaments, which he tended to regard as his own personal cat toys. They had also discouraged him, countless times, from climbing up into the tree, afraid that he might get tangled in the LED lights and get electrocuted. But this year was different. Sweetie-Pete didn't seem to want any part of the new tree whatsoever.

Jordan took her iPhone out of her hip pocket and checked the time. "Crap! It's already four-thirty! We've got to get this tree decorated for Dad before he calls!"

"Calm down," her mother said. "We've got plenty of time. You kids fetch the ornaments from the hall closet and I'll heat up that leftover chili from the other night and make us some grilled cheeses. We'll play some Christmas music and have a big tree-trimming party before the call comes in."

Excited, Danny and Jordan ran to the closet to begin toting

the lights and ornaments to the living room. As Kim passed
the sofa, she reached out to run an affectionate hand down the
tabby's back. Sweetie-Pete dodged her hand and continued his
pacing, cutting his eyes toward the tree every now and then.
"What's up with you, mister?" she asked, then headed to
the kitchen to prepare supper.

That night, at eight minutes after nine, they were still waiting
in front of the laptop for Nick Ballard's Skype to come through.
"You don't think they're having a sandstorm or something
do you?" asked Danny. There was a tone of doom and dejection
in his voice. "They always play havoc with the Internet. I've been
waiting for this all day!"
"We all have, honey," Kim assured him. "He's just running
late. Probably had a lot of other soldiers ahead of him. Most of
them aren't coming home for the holidays like he is. They deserve
a little extra time with their calls."
"I know, Mom. It's just that I miss him *so* much!"
Me and you both, she thought to herself. *More than you can
imagine.*
Movement in the little box in the middle of the monitor
screen drew their attention and, suddenly, a familiar face was
smiling at them from seven thousand miles away. Strong, dark-
haired, tanned from months in the Middle Eastern sun...sort of
like Superman in desert fatigues.
"Ballard clan...fall in!" he commanded in his best drill
sergeant voice.
A mutual cheer went up among the three. "Hey, Dad!"
greeted the boy, excitedly. "How's it going?"
"It'll be going a lot better when I'm on that long flight back to
Tennessee. Is everyone ready for an incredible Christmas?"
"You bet!"
"Fantastic! So am I."
"Look, Dad!" said Jordan. "Look at the tree!" The three
shifted out of the way so that he could see the gleaming tree
with the angel on top.
"Whoa!" said Nick, his eyes bulging with exaggerated awe.
"I didn't know you were going to drive all the way to California

and bring back a giant Sequoia."

"Do you like it, sweetheart?" Kim asked. She felt both sad and gloriously happy at the same time.

Nick's smile faltered for an instant and she knew he was feeling the same way. "It's absolutely wonderful, baby. I can't wait for us to roll around underneath it and suck face all over the Christmas gifts."

Jordan clamped her hands over her reddening ears. "Dad! Stop it...please!"

As they all laughed, Danny grabbed the cat and shoved him into the screen.

"Someone else misses you, too!"

The cat had no interest in the man on the computer screen. He attempted to climb over the ten-year-old's shoulder, doing his best to keep the far end of the living room in sight.

"What's up with ol' Pete?" asked Nick.

"Oh, he's been acting like a big goofball all evening," Kim told him. "I don't know what's going on with him."

She was about to ask her husband if he was all packed, when a peculiar expression crossed his face. His smile faded and he looked a little surprised. He even leaned a little closer to the screen. It took Kim a moment, but she realized that he was no longer looking at them...but directly behind them.

"What's wrong, Nick?"

"Oh...nothing," he said. His smile returned, but his eyes were still searching. "Nothing at all. Just thought I saw the tree *move*."

Kim and the children turned and looked behind them. The branches seemed to be in the same, stationary position that they had been since the twine had been cut, but a couple of ornaments in the middle were swinging ever so slightly on their wire hooks.

Their attention was drawn back to the screen when a gruff voice said "Ballard, time's up. Shut 'er down."

"Right, Major," Nick replied and turned a sad, hang-dog face toward his family. He pouted, making them laugh. "I don't wanna go."

"You'll see us soon enough and then you'll be sick and tired of us," his daughter told him. Her voice cracked and she shifted her head a little, so he wouldn't see her cry.

"Be at Metro Airport in Nashville at 1400 hours next Tuesday to pick me up," he said, flashing that infectious smile again. "I love you all."

"We love you, too!" All three in unison, in voice and heart.

"Ballard!"

"The CO calls," laughed Nick. "Gotta go." And then the connection went dark.

They sat in the living room in silence for a long moment, then Kim said, "Who wants hot chocolate with marshmallows?"

The desire for liquid candy was unanimous. Their spirits lifted as they headed to the kitchen, laughing and planning to snack and wrap presents until bedtime.

And, stretched out on the arm of the sofa, Sweetie-Pete watched the tree.

Kim got up the next morning to find that someone had torn the angel tree topper to shreds.

It lay on the floor in a dozen pieces. The porcelain head and arms were shattered into sharp bits and the gown of the body torn into thin shreds and scattered all over the carpet, along with the dislodged feathers of its wings.

"Well, shit!" She crouched and examined the keepsake, which had belonged to her mother and her mother before her. "Dumb old cat."

"What's up, Mom?" Danny yawned as he entered the living room in his pajamas. The orange tabby followed closely on his heels.

"Oh, Sweetie-Pete got up in the tree last night and went postal on the angel," she told him. She glared at the cat. "Bad boy!"

The boy shook his cow-licked head. "Uh-uh. Pete slept on the foot of my bed all night...and my door was closed."

Kim looked down at the murdered cherubim. "Well, it didn't get this way by falling off." It was silly to even think it, but it almost looked as if there had been some malice and contempt behind the destruction...as though the perpetrator had a hatred for God's heavenly attendants.

"Mom...I think we have mice in the house." Jordan walked into the living room. She was beginning her morning ritual as usual, tapping at her phone and checking her Snapchat and Twitter.

"Really? How come?"

The girl shrugged. "I heard scratching at my bedroom door last night. Or gnawing...it was hard to tell."

"Sweetheart, a mouse could squeeze through the gap beneath your door," Kim told her. "Why would it scratch on it?"

"Gee, Mom, I don't know. I'm not a freaking mouse, am I?"

The mangled tree topper had soured Kim's mood that morning. "Watch the tone, sass-britches!"

The teenager looked up from her phone. "Uh, sorry." Her eyes widened when she saw the mess on the floor. "What happened to Nanny's angel? Did it crash and burn?"

"I thought Pete climbed up and attacked it, but I'm not sure now. Maybe it did just fall off."

Jordan shook her head, looking as puzzled as her mother. "And exploded when it hit the floor? I don't think so."

Kim glanced toward the hallway. The hands on the grandfather clock spelled out seven forty-five. "Hon, could you get a broom and a dustpan and clean this up? I have a house to show at nine-thirty and I'm running late." She looked over at her son. "Danny, get me a bowl of cereal, will you? I'll pour the milk when I get out of the shower."

The boy nodded and shuffled sleepily toward the kitchen. "Froot Loops or Cocoa Pebbles?"

She had just about overdosed on chocolate the night before. "Loops."

"After breakfast, can I climb back into bed for a while? Remember, no school. It's Christmas break."

"Okay," she allowed, heading down the hallway to the master bathroom. "But don't sleep half the day away. There's a list of chores for you and your sister on the refrigerator."

Jordan rolled her eyes. "Isn't there always?"

"Tone, young lady...tone!"

"Sorry!" But she smiled to herself when her mother was out of sight.

Kim stopped before she made it halfway down the hall. She crouched and studied the bottom of Jordan's bedroom door. There were long furrows scored into the wood...not at the very bottom, but a quarter of the way toward the center panel.

Have you turned into Houdini, Sweetie-Pete? she wondered.

It was the only explanation she could come up with, but not one that set with her very well.

Kim and the couple from Nashville walked up the paved driveway, past the Blackwood Realty sign, to the two-story spec house on Timber Ridge Drive. She was hoping for a quick sell and signed commitment. More and more people from Music City were moving out to the country to avoid crime and high property taxes.

They were halfway to the front walk when the woman, Karen Moore, looked past her, in the direction of the neighbor's property. "Who is that?"

Kim looked over, suddenly feeling embarrassed, afraid that the man picking through the trash can near the street would somehow ruin her sales pitch. Then she immediately felt ashamed of herself. It was just old Hot Pappy.

Jeremiah Springer, known throughout the county as "Hot Pappy" because of his rambling, womanizing ways during his youth, was something of a sad joke in the community of Pikesville. He had been arrested for public drunkenness dozens of times and seemed to spend more time in the county jail than out. The elderly black man was short and wiry, with curly white hair and a beard to match. His bloodshot eyes—one lazy and canted slightly to the left—were a peculiar shade of slate gray. His teeth were crooked and stained a yellowish brown with tobacco juice. He was dressed in a dirty orange University of Tennessee ball cap, a winter coat that looked three sizes too large for him, and a pair of patched blue jeans.

Some folks in Pikesville disliked the old man, but Kim had always felt badly for him and his situation. When he was sober, Hot Pappy could be found making a dollar here and there, doing odd jobs around town and collecting aluminum cans wherever he could find them. That was what he was up to that morning—scrounging for cans to sell at the junkyard…for drinking money, more than likely.

"Oh, that's just Hot Pappy," she told them matter-of-factly. *Just forget it*, she thought, as if mentally willing the couple to turn away. *You want to see this house don't you?*

But, unfortunately, they wouldn't. "Does he hang around here often?" Brad Moore wanted to know. The young attorney looked as though someone had just tossed a dead dog at his feet.

"Oh, people around here don't seem to mind him going through their trash. He's just looking for cans. He never leaves a mess or anything."

"Well, *we* mind," said Karen. "Can't the police do anything about him? A homeless man wandering around a nice neighborhood like this?"

Kim felt her temper rise. She was beginning to believe that the couple's suspicions had more to do with the color of his skin than the fact that he was digging through the trash. "Oh, he's not homeless. He's got a little place of his own. He's sort of a jack-of-all-trades. I've seen him doing all kinds of jobs around town."

"Well, I'm not sure if this is the place for us, if we constantly have to be on the lookout for…"

Don't say "undesirables". Please…just don't.

"…unfortunate souls like that."

"I told you we should look for a gated community," Brad told his wife.

Kim was beginning to believe a potential commission wasn't worth the effort, especially where these jerks were concerned. *There are no gated communities in Pikesville, you assholes!*, she wanted to tell them. But she simply kept her smile firmly in place, as much as it hurt to do so.

"Why don't we go inside and take a look at the house," she suggested.

The couple stared at the elderly man one last time, before turning their eyes back to the house. "Well…okay."

As they walked up the steps to the front door, Kim looked back at Hot Pappy. She was surprised to see him looking straight at them. He grinned and directed a bony, black middle finger at the two young professionals, then gave Kim a wry wink.

She couldn't help but smile and nod in agreement. *Exactly what I was thinking.*

Then they both went back to what they had been doing that cold, December morning.

For the next couple of days, an odd sensation of dread seemed to settle in the Ballard household.

They should have been excited in anticipation for their husband and father's return, but some odd occurrences around the house put a damper on that feeling. All three began to get the feeling that something had gotten into the house...maybe a rat from the landfill down the road, or a raccoon or possum from the woods out back. How it would have made its way into the house undetected, they had no idea.

Deep scratches had appeared on all of the bedroom doors, a little higher than the ones Kim had initially discovered on Jordan's. And there were a couple of scratches on the brass of the doorknobs as well.

They had also found shattered ornaments around the Christmas tree and the wrapping paper of a few presents torn open. They all knew it wasn't Sweetie-Pete. He slept with either Danny or Jordan at night, with the door closed.

"This is starting to freak me out, Mom," Jordan told her on the third day, but not in front of her little brother.

"I hate to admit it, but me, too," Kim replied. "I'll call someone in the morning...an exterminator or county animal control. Maybe find someone who can find whatever it is and get it the hell out of here."

That night, Kim awoke to a noise in the kitchen.

She heard a rattle like pots and pans shifting, followed by something falling from a kitchen cabinet, rolling across a counter, and hitting the floor with a thud. *Okay, let's see what's going on,* she thought, reaching into the nightstand drawer and finding the Taurus 9mm that Nick kept there.

Kim slipped out of bed and walked, barefooted, to her bedroom door. She paused for a long moment, listening. *Was I dreaming?* Then, another clatter and something that sounded like clawed feet skittering across the granite countertop.

She opened her door and stepped into the hallway. Another rattle…silverware in a drawer? *Don't wake up, kids. Don't wake up.*

As she passed Jordan's bedroom door, a scratching drew her attention.

She spun and aimed the pistol downward.

Meow

She crouched and lowered a hand to the gap beneath the door. Sweetie-Pete's paw appeared and stroked her fingers. "Quiet, boy," she whispered. "I've got this." *I hope.*

Kim straightened up and continued down the hallway to the kitchen. She held the 9mm in a two-fisted grip. She was no stranger to the gun, having qualified with the weapon and logged hours at the firing range with it. Still, the thought of actually firing it inside the house, at only God knew what, was unnerving to say the least.

She reached the kitchen, stepped through the doorway, and peeked around the corner of the refrigerator. Moonlight shone through the single window over the sink, sending pale swaths of light across the room. From where she stood, she could see that about all of the cabinet doors were open and most of the contents were scattered across the counters and floor.

Where are you? her thoughts screamed. *Where the hell are you, you sneaky little bastard?*

Then abruptly, one of the cabinet doors next to the sink slowly swung open and something stepped out.

As it turned out, the culprit wasn't little at all.

It crouched in the shadows beyond the moonglow, its eyes— the size and shape of small lemons—gleaming dull yellow in the gloom. She couldn't make the thing's features out very well because of the darkness, but it was big. About the size of a young golden retriever, but longer and leaner in nature. And there was a peculiar shine to its black coat…almost a gleam or sparkle.

Her hand trembled as she reached for the light switch and snapped it on. Nothing. She looked at the floor and saw brittle shards of glass lying about. It had busted the kitchen light. *Oh God…what is this thing?*

A low noise sounded from the thing…a deep guttural growl

that rose in pitch, ending in a shrill hiss. She noticed its nimble back rising, arching…its muscles tensing.

Shoot it! Shoot the damned thing!

She caressed the curve of the trigger with her index finger and prepared to squeeze.

Before she could, the thing in the shadows made a quick turn and rushed through the opposite door. From where she stood, Kim could see the Christmas tree. They had a tradition of keeping it lit at night, even after bedtime. It stood, tall and broad, its LED lights glowing in primary colors of red, blue, green, and yellow. The dark creature scampered down the hall, low to the floor, then sprang and hit the tree. The pine rocked on its stand for a moment as the thing burrowed into the thick branches. The last thing she saw—or *thought* she saw—was a long, black tail withdrawing into the shelter of the branches, then disappearing from sight.

Kim turned and ran for the kids' bedrooms. The first one she entered was Jordan's. The instant she opened the door, Sweetie-Pete shot out, like a flash, between her ankles. "Get back here, Pete!" she called, but the cat was already through the kitchen and into the living room.

Jordan sat up in bed, startled. "What's going on?"

"Get dressed! We've got to get out of here. There's something in the house!'

"Well, duh…we already know that."

"Something *big*…like a dog." She remembered the long, black tail disappearing into the dense heart of the tree and almost said *alligator.*

"How did a freaking dog get in—?"

"Shut up and get your clothes on!" Kim screamed at her, immediately regretting the edge in her voice. She realized that she was near hysteria. "I'll get Danny."

A moment later, she was rousing the boy from a sound sleep. "Is it Christmas yet?" he mumbled groggily.

"No, sweetheart." She found his sneakers next to his bed and slipped them over his bare feet. "We're just going to spend the night at Grandma's."

"How come?"

Kim stepped to his chest of drawers and found some clothes

to take with her. "Because I said so." She picked out a sweatshirt, jeans, underwear, and socks.

"Mom." Jordan was standing at her brother's doorway, fully awake now. "Why are you holding that gun?" Frightened, she turned and looked toward the living room and the brightly-lit tree that stood beside the fireplace. "You weren't kidding, were you?"

"Kidding about what?" Danny sat on the edge of his bed, looking like he wanted to lie down and go back to sleep.

"Can you carry your brother?" Kim asked her daughter.

"Do I look like Dad or something?" Jordan stared at her mother like she was crazy. "He weighs ninety pounds now. He's not a four-year-old anymore, you know."

"We'll go to the car through the utility room." Kim ushered her children from the bedroom and all three swiftly made their way down the hallway. She held the Taurus ahead of her, prepared to fire if something came at them out of the darkness.

"What about Pete?" Jordan asked shrilly.

"Lower your voice, dear. I have no idea where he went. I'll come back and get him… after I take you to your grandmother's."

A moment later, they were through the back door of the utility room and outside. The temperature had dropped past freezing before midnight and it was snowing, although nothing was on the driveway or road yet. They climbed into Kim's Murano and buckled up.

All three were dead silent as the SUV backed into the street and headed for the north side of town.

Kim returned at six o'clock in the morning.

Gray clouds still spit snow, adding a light layer to drifts that had compounded to three inches over the past few hours. Kim parked next to the back door, took the 9mm from where it lay on the passenger seat, and left the vehicle.

The house was silent. The only thing she heard was the steady *tick-tick-tick* of the grandfather clock. She stepped out of the utility room and into the hallway that linked the living room to the bedrooms.

"Pete," she called softly. "Sweetie-Pete…where are you?"

Still no sound. It was gloomy in the house with only the pale light of dawn filtering through the curtains of the windows. The Christmas tree stood where it had before, the lights still glowing.

Kim took a chance and turned on the hallway light. She saw it immediately…several drops of blood and a tuft of orange fluff on the carpet in front of the half-bathroom. The door was partially open and it was dark inside.

"Pete?" Still gripping the gun in the combat hold Nick had taught her, Kim pushed the door the rest of the way open. She stepped cautiously inside and flipped the light switch with her right elbow.

A sound came from over her head. A dry, rasping sound.

She looked toward the ceiling and nearly screamed.

There, attached to the light fixture, was some sort of bag…or cocoon…about the size of a large purse. It seemed to be translucent in nature. Kim thought it was made of silk or webbing at first, but then she saw the scaly texture of the chrysalis. *Is that…is that snakeskin?*

The thing revolved slowly from the leathery cable that attached it to the fixture. It shuddered and twitched slightly, and a soft sound came from inside.

Mew.

Kim's heart sank. *Oh God! Oh, dear Jesus….*

It made another lazy half-turn and stopped. That's when she saw what was inside.

It was Sweetie-Pete.

Without thinking, she laid the gun on the vanity and reached up. Her fingertips barely brushed the bottom of the cocoon. She remembered the little stepping stool beneath the sink, the one she had stashed away when Danny grew big enough to brush his teeth without needing something to stand on. She pulled it out and, positioning it in the center of the bathroom floor, stepped up and took hold of the pouch. It was dry and rough to the touch. She could see the orange tabby inside, eyes closed, his legs and tail folded around him. Kim expected to feel warmth through the cocoon, but it felt alarmingly cool.

She tried her best to keep calm, but she couldn't help but cry. *He's dying.*

Kim tugged at the bag with all her strength. It held firm at first, then the elastic that held it aloft began to stretch and weaken. The light fixture creaked and she was certain that she would pull the whole thing on top of her head. Then it broke loose with a *snap* and she held it in her hands.

Through the transparent hide, Sweetie-Pete opened his eyes. They were dull and glazed. Then he closed them again.

"Don't worry, buddy," she whispered. "I'm taking you to the vet."

She cradled the cocooned cat in the crook of her left arm and picked the pistol up with her right hand. Then she stepped out into the hallway and walked to where the corridor gave way to the family room.

She stared at the tree for a long moment, before she saw movement in the center, within a gap in the branches. She detected the gleam of glossy blackness and those two yellow eyes with the narrow-slitted pupils.

"I'm coming back, you son of a bitch," she told it. "I'm coming back...and I'm going to kill your ass."

The yellow eyes narrowed a bit and a low hiss sounded. She couldn't see its lower face or mouth, but almost knew it was smiling in its own sinister way.

As Kim backed away, she suddenly knew whom to turn to. Someone that might be able to help Sweetie-Pete better than a veterinarian. And maybe help her deal with *this* as well. She remembered something her father had said when she was child, one sunny Sunday morning as they drove to church and passed a man staggering along the sidewalk, drunk as a skunk.

Sure...he has his problems. He can certainly outdrink a school of catfish. But he has knowledge, too. Knowledge of things you and I could never imagine. Otherworldly things. Especially if they stray across the county line.

The door of the old shack opened at Kim's third knock.

The old man seemed surprised to see her. "Mrs. Ballard?"

She held the thing from the ceiling out to him. "Please..."

could you help me with this?"

Hot Pappy looked down at the snakeskin cocoon. "Good God Almighty!" He reached out with bony hands and gently took it from her. "Come inside."

Kim stood there, heart pounding, as he took the cocoon to an old kitchen table that looked as though it had come from the county landfill. He laid it on the surface and took a pocketknife from his pants pocket. "Open that cabinet on the wall yonder," he instructed. "There's a jar with a pink powder with yellow grains mixed in. There's an eye dropper next to it."

As Hot Pappy extended the longest and sharpest blade, Kim ran to the cabinet and looked for what he needed. There were hundreds of jars, tins, and bottles on the cabinet's five shelves. They all contained various powders and liquids, dried berries, and roots. She found the one he described. "Is this it?"

He nodded as he carefully inserted the tip of the knife into the top of the pod and began to run the edge downward. "Go to the fridge. There's half a gallon of milk there. Pour half a cup in one of those jelly jar glasses by the sink and mix a tablespoon of that powder in. Stir it up good. Then bring it and that dropper over here."

She did as he instructed. When she reached the table with the mixture, the cocoon had been laid in half. He pulled the sides away and tenderly lifted the cat from its imprisonment. Kim was stunned. Sweetie-Pete looked small and shriveled, like he had lost two or three pounds. He was limp and lethargic, and his orange-striped coat held streaks of white, as though bleached from sheer shock.

"What's wrong with him?" she gasped.

Hot Pappy took the dropper and drew it full of pink milk. He forced the tip past the cat's lips. At first, it wanted no part of it. But, it soon began to suck from the stem.

"He's been fed upon," the old man told her. "Cinched up in that damnable sack and pert near drained of blood and spirit." He looked at the woman, his bloodshot eyes solemn. "What did this?" he asked, although the grimness in his face revealed that he already knew.

"It's in my house," she said. "I think we brought it in with the

Christmas tree."

As Hot Pappy attended to the feline, Sweetie-Pete began to stretch, his limbs growing less rigid. "The potion…it's neutralizing the toxins. The thing that bit him paralyzes its prey and imprisons it, to feed on it in its own good time." He looked over at her. "This Christmas tree…where did you get it? Across the river?"

Kim suddenly felt foolish. "Yes. From a man selling them at the side of the road."

"An odd, little fellow with dark eyes and a mouth that frowned and smiled at the same time?"

"Yes! That's him."

The black man nodded. "I know of the man. Not the kind of person I'd trust to do business with."

Kim realized that now. "Will Pete be okay?"

"We'll leave him here to rest and recuperate," Hot Pappy told her. His wrinkled features seemed to tighten at the jaw and around the eyes. "While we take care of your problem at home."

"Can you do that?" she asked.

"Yes, but I'll need help. I know someone who can."

He took a blanket from an old armchair that was busted at the seams and held together with silver duct tape. Hot Pappy wrapped the cat in the warm folds of the throw and left him in the seat of the chair. Sweetie-Pete slept peacefully and breathed easily.

Kim watched as the old man took a leather bag and filled it with several jars and bottles. "Ammunition for the battle to come," he explained, shouldering the satchel and placing the baseball cap on his head.

"Hot Pappy…I just want to…."

He sensed what she was about to say. "You can thank me later…when the dragon is slain."

Together, they walked out to Kim's vehicle and headed in the direction that Hot Pappy told her.

When they got there, a strange feeling gripped Kim.

"Do you know where we are?" he asked her.

"Yes." She pulled into the gravel driveway and parked a few yards from the old farmhouse. "I do."

Hot Pappy got out, taking the leather bag with him. "You go on back home and wait for us outside."

She nodded. "So, it's true. All the old stories."

The old black man didn't say yes or no. "Remember, wait for us and don't go inside until we get there."

As Kim backed the Murano out of the driveway, Hot Pappy trudged across the snowy yard and mounted the steps to the front porch. He paused for a moment, then knocked on the door.

A tall, silver-haired man answered. He stood in the doorway and regarded Hot Pappy warily. "This isn't a good time. My grandkids are visiting."

The expression of grim determination in the black man's bearded face didn't flinch. "I hear you still have a keen eye and a steady hand."

The man at the door stood there silently for a moment more. Then he said, "Let me fetch my coat."

Hot Pappy watched through the doorway as the man opened the closet door and slipped on a denim jacket. Then he reached for a shoebox on the top shelf, took something out, and slipped it in his pocket.

"Who was that, sweetheart?" a woman's voice called from the kitchen. The rich scent of bacon and pancakes filled the house.

"Just someone who needs a helping hand, Mandy," he called back. "I'll be back in a little while."

He shut the door behind him, and together—silently—the two climbed into the man's Chevy pickup and headed across town for the Ballard place.

They entered the house together.

Hot Pappy went first, then the man with the silver hair. Kim followed behind them. She had started to bring the 9mm pistol with her, but the old black man had dissuaded her. "Best leave that in your car," he had told her. "If you think you can punch a hole in that thing with a bullet, you're mistaken."

They walked through the house quietly, until they reached the living room. A few glass ornaments had fallen to the floor and shattered, but that was the only sign of disturbance that could be detected.

"I smell it," said Hot Pappy, his nostrils flaring.

"So do I," said the other man. "It's a smell you never forget."

Kim suddenly knew what they were talking about. The strong, earthy smell that she had noticed when they brought the tree into the house, plus something more...a musky, rancid odor like the stench of some reptilian beast. A lyric to an old John Prine song came to mind...the one about the air smelling like snakes.

Something in the tree shifted. Then that deep-throated growl that rose and transcended into a shrill, breathy hissing.

"Stand back there in the hallway, Mrs. Ballard," Hot Pappy instructed. "If anything goes wrong...*run.*"

She watched as the two men walked past the sofa to the center of the living room and stopped ten feet from the Christmas tree. They stood side by side, Hot Pappy to the left, the man in the denim jacket to the right. Hot Pappy set the leather bag at his feet and removed two objects. One was a vial of pale blue powder. The other was a small pint Mason jar with a single object inside.

The black man unscrewed the lid of the jar, then handed the taller man its contents. From where Kim stood, it looked like a small chicken egg, but pitch black in color. The man cradled the object in his left hand and reached into his jacket pocket on the right. Kim was surprised at what he brought into view. It was a crude slingshot made from a fragment of forked oak branch with a broad strip of inner tube stretched and tied from one arm to the other. It looked more like something a young boy would carry, rather than a man in his early eighties.

Both men looked at one another and nodded. Hot Pappy uncapped the vial and poured a generous fistful of blue powder into his dark palm. The one next to him took the black egg, placed it in the center of the rubber tubing, and held it there, ready to lift and aim when the time came.

Hot Pappy opened his mouth and unleashed an uncanny imitation of the creature in the tree. A low, rumbling growl that rose in pitch and intensity until it cut through their ears like a shrill hiss.

The tree wobbled on its base and the thick branches thrashed wildly, dislodging ornaments, which either rolled across the carpet or shattered into jagged shards. *Whatever that thing is*, thought Kim, *he's really pissed it off.*

Hot Pappy cleared his throat and issued the call again. This time there was a different tone and resonance to it, and the hiss came in a quick, taunting staccato.

Apparently, that was too much for the thing in the tree to bear. It tore past the branches of its concealment and landed, in a defiant crouch, seven feet away from them.

It was a horrifying creature, about six feet long from blunted snout to tail, and covered with thick, ebony scales. It resembled a cross between a snake and a dog, except that it was low to the ground and its legs were lean and nimble. Its feet were long-fingered and tipped with sharp, black claws that were hooked at the ends. The eyes that she had seen staring at her from behind the boughs of the tree were huge, yellow, and serpentine...now brimming with malice and bad intent.

"Get ready," Hot Pappy said softly.

The tall man nodded and pulled the band of the slingshot to capacity. "I am." There was a rigid determination in his aged face, but also the fear of a child in his eyes.

Hot Pappy shrieked at the creature again. In response, it raised its head and opened its wicked jaws wide, showing jagged yellow teeth set in black gums. The fangs that had incapacitated Sweetie-Pete dripped thick green venom. It let out a long, ear-piercing screech that belied an evil that Kim had only imagined could exist, but only now encountered firsthand.

When the creature's jaws were stretched to their limit, Hot Pappy flung the handful of blue powder. It hit the monster squarely in the face. Then a funny thing happened. It jerked and grew rigid, freezing in place. Whatever the powder was, it had paralyzed the thing, if only temporarily.

"*Now!*" hollered Hot Pappy at the top of his lungs.

The silver-haired man lifted the slingshot, aimed, and released. The projectile was a quick, black blur as it traveled from the cradle of the makeshift weapon and landed deep in the glistening tunnel of the creature's throat.

They watched as the creature began to move again, sluggishly at first, then quicker as the effects of the powder wore off. It took one step forward, then stopped. It shook its scaly head violently as blackish-blue smoke began to seep from between its fangs and the small pits of its nostrils. The brilliant yellow eyes dulled, changing into a reddish-orange hue. It staggered forward a couple more steps, then dropped heavily to the floor. It howled in defeat as the muscles beneath the shiny black flesh began to break down and shrink. The monster opened its mouth and moaned. Its reptilian eyes sank back into its skull and its fangs began to drop from its gums, one by one.

The three solemnly stood there and watched its demise. It began to curl into itself. A dusty, dry odor like ancient and forgotten things in an attic replaced the sharp scent of snake. Then, with one final wheeze, the thing was gone.

Kim walked into the living room and stood over its shriveled remains. "What the hell was it?"

"A snake-critter," Hot Pappy told her. "A young female."

"What was it doing in the tree?"

"In the winter months, they leave the canebrake and hibernate in the forests…find themselves a tree and nestle flat against the trunk. Feed on squirrels and birds unfortunate enough to live there," he explained. "And the bastard who sold you this tree knew it. Either he didn't give a damn or he did it on purpose. Folks yonder way tend to have nothing but evil and ill intentions in their dark hearts."

"But…why the egg?"

Hot Pappy picked up the empty jar, replaced the lid, and put it back in the leather satchel. "The only thing that can kill a snake-critter is devouring its own kind. Using a critter egg is a solution my grandmother came up with."

She turned and, without hesitation, hugged the man known as the town drunk of Pikesville. "Thank you, Jeremiah. Thank you for what you did for Pete…and me and my family."

At the sound of his given name, which he hadn't heard aloud in quite a while, the man relaxed and patted her on the back. "I'm always of service, Mrs. Ballard. It was what I was raised to do. I went into the heart of darkness once, for my schooling."

She could imagine the place he was referring to. She stepped back and then moved to the old man in the denim jacket. Silver-haired, tall, and strong as an oak. She had practically known the man since she was born. He had been a loyal friend of the family...a hunting buddy and good friend of her paternal grandfather.

"Thanks for coming to my rescue," she said with tears in her eyes. She embraced him tightly. "I should have believed all those tall tales you told me when I was a little girl."

Jeb Sweeny smiled and hugged her back. "Couldn't let my little Kimmie face something like this alone," he told her. "And I'm sorry you had to find out the truth of those stories the hard way."

She turned to find Hot Pappy on his hands and knees, beneath her Christmas tree, rooting through the gifts. He paused at one and pulled away a flap of wrapping paper that had come loose. There was a good-sized hole in the side of the box. The man stuck his hand inside and nodded. When he stood up, he held the present in his hands.

"Who does this gift belong to?" he asked her.

"My husband's Aunt Betty. Just some dish towels and pot-holders that the kids picked out."

"So, it can be easily replaced...and I can take this one with me?"

She had no idea why he wanted it, but figured it was for a good reason. "Sure. No problem."

Hot Pappy nodded and tucked the present under his arm. "If you fetch a trash bag, we'll help you clean up. These critters don't die easily, but when they do, they leave one nasty, godawful mess."

The two men were silent as they headed for a destination neither one was anxious to reach.

Halfway there, Jeb asked a question that had been nagging him. "What's inside the box?"

Hot Pappy looked down at the brightly-wrapped present that sat on the seat between them. "A nest. Seven eggs in all. As cold as a stone in a winter creek bed, but close to term." He looked at the man behind the wheel. "I'd drive a little faster, if I were you. I'd hate for these things to hatch while we were still in here."

Minutes later, they crossed the Cumberland River Bridge and parked at the side of the road. They sat and stared at the sign that stood thirty yards away. It was battered and rusty, riddled with buckshot and bullet holes, but readable. WELCOME TO FEAR COUNTY.

The heater of the truck was going full-blast, but still the two men felt an aching cold chill them to the marrow of their aged bones.

"You'll have to take it," Jeb told him. "I promised myself many years ago that I'd never cross that line again, and I ain't about to change my mind now."

Hot Pappy sighed. He looked down at the box, then at the dense forest beyond the road sign. "You knew my grandmother, didn't you?"

Jeb smiled warmly. "The Granny Woman."

The black man nodded. "She taught me everything I know… in Paradise Hollow, smack dab in the middle of that evil, godless place. Said there had to be someone to take her place…someone to stand tall against that damnable county in case the badness broke past its borders and spilled over. It's not a job I take lightly. I reckon that's why I drown my fears in drink so often."

"I feel badly for you," the elderly man told him. "At least I have a choice to steer clear. You never did."

Something inside the Christmas gift moved.

"I reckon I'd best take them home," he said. Hot Pappy picked up the box and left the truck.

It had started to flurry again. Snowflakes drifted from the gray sky overhead. He reached the sign, crouched, and placed the gift at its base.

He couldn't help but smile scornfully at the wilderness that stretched before him. "Merry Christmas!" he called out loudly.

Hot Pappy could feel contemptuous eyes on him, full of poison and hatred, from the dark columns of the trees and the dense thicket that lay in between. They knew who he was…knew his capabilities and the damage he could wreak on them and the dark realm they called home.

As he turned and headed back to the truck, he heard the crisp ripping of wrapping paper behind him.

Without hesitation, he quickened his pace and walked a little faster.

PAPA'S EXILE

"Will Papa come home for Christmas?" asks Stephanie, her face staring hopefully from amid the snug safety of her pillows, blankets, and plush stuffed animals.

"I'm afraid not," says Mother. She reaches down and brushes a stray curl from her daughter's brow.

"Won't he never, ever come home again?"

Mother shakes her head. "No, dear. Never again."

Stephanie begins to ask why, but the dousing of the light curtails that simple question. "Sweet dreams, my darling, and Merry Christmas," Mother whispers and leaves her with a kiss.

The wind begins to howl, heralding the approach of a winter's squall, as Mother walks the darkened halls of the old house. Her daughter's question brings a thin smile to her lips and she pauses by the parlor window. The persimmon grove crowds against the northern wall. Skeletal sentries stand tall and somber, as if ever watching.

No, never again. Not her dear, half-blind husband. Never again would his drunken voice resound within their peaceful household, eliciting fear and dread, nor would there be the fleshy blows of anger. And his mustachioed face would never glare hatefully across the dinner table, one eye livid, the other emotionless, unreal.

Never again will you rule us, she had told him that awful Christmas night a year ago…a night laced with pain and the raw stench of liquor. Never again will you find comfort before the warmth of the hearth, nor in the folds of our marriage bed. Never again shall you savor the scent of my perfume or relish the softness of my skin.

She had declared all of these things and they had come to

pass. After that winter night, Papa no longer filled the gabled structure with his troublesome presence...no longer darkened the cobbled walk with his weaving, drunken shadow.

The storm comes, forceful and born of vengeance. Dark clouds boil overhead, advancing, engulfing the land with their surly discontent. Snow falls, first gently, then swirling, growing in both density and intensity. Beside the house, the grove dances, swaying to and fro, trees animated.

Amid the fury of the blizzard, something winks, reflecting the candlelight of the parlor Christmas tree. Then, as a violent and icy gust sweeps the grove, it falls like a lone hailstone, bounces, rolls across the snow-laden carpet of night.

Christmas morning reigns supreme.

Young Stephanie, bundled and warm against the cold, strolls down the snowy pathway through Mother's garden, pushing the baby buggy that Saint Nicholas had left beside the tree the night before. Beneath a pink blanket, a china doll with golden hair snuggles, immersed in porcelain dreams.

As Stephanie leaves the garden and journeys into the persimmon grove, she marvels at the winter wonderland before her—the snow as clean and white as Mother's baking flour, the crystal fangs of icicles hanging high upon limbs and branches. As she travels through the leafless columns, she is suddenly teased by an earthward sparkle. Stephanie spies a glistening orb lying at the foot of an ancient tree, hollow and dead from the ravages of time. Picking up the peculiar object, she polishes it against the cloth of her winter coat...marveling, a treasure to behold.

She stares at it and it stares back. Familiar, yet unreal.

Curiously, the girl regards the old tree, for the trunk's gaping seam has been opened further by the angry passing of the gale. As she draws nearer, something within the hollow shifts and falls forward.

Stephanie squeals, but not in delight.

Papa has come home.

THE PEDDLERS JOURNEY

"Tell us, Grandpa!"

Chester McCorkendale shared his little brother's enthusiasm. "Yeah, come on, Grandpa," he urged, sitting on the threadbare rug before the hearth. "Tell us the story about the Ghostly Peddler!"

Grandpa eyed the boys with ancient eyes and smiled. He took a puff on the briar pipe he clutched in yellowed dentures and let the blue smoke roll from his nostrils like dragon's breath. "Ah, you boys have heard that old tale every Christmas Eve since you were knee-high to a grasshopper."

"But we want to hear it again," David demanded. "It's like a...you know, whaddaya call it?"

"Tradition," his big brother told him. "Come on, Grandpa. Nobody tells it like you do."

Grandpa McCorkendale chuckled and leaned back in his hickory wood rocker, causing it to creak dryly. He glanced around the cramped main room of the cabin. The crackling fire cast a warm, orange glow over the walls papered with newsprint, the stones of the hearth, and the long, dangling stockings that drooped from the mantle—stockings that had been darned by their Ma a half-dozen times or so. Yes, this was the place to tell the old story again, and most certainly the time.

Grandpa couldn't help but string them along a bit further, though. "Are you sure you want ghost stories and not 'The Night Before Christmas' or the birth of Jesus? I'll just go filling your head full of haints and horrors, and you boys'll never get to sleep tonight."

"Are you gonna tell it or what?" snapped David, rolling his eyes.

Chester elbowed his brother sharply. He didn't want David to cross the fine line between childish pestering and disrespecting an elder. That was one thing Grandpa, no matter how patient he was, would not tolerate. There was no need to go fishing for a hide-tanning...especially on Christmas Eve.

Grandpa's eyes sparkled. "All right. I won't leave you waiting any longer. Your Ma and Pa's done gone to bed, and you'd best get nestled beneath the quilts yourself." He grinned around the stem of his pipe. "Besides, if Ol' Saint Nick can't make it this year, 'cause of this dadblamed Depression and all, then the Ghostly Peddler might just show up, bearing gifts."

The very thought of the mountain ghost standing before their hearth sent a delicious chill shivering through their bones. They lay on their bellies on the rug, their chins planted in their palms, waiting for the storyteller to begin.

Grandpa puffed on his pipe a moment more, staring almost dreamily into the blue haze of tobacco smoke. "They say it happened in the winter of 1869. The cannons that echoed violently down in the valley during the War Betwixt the States had scarcely been silent four years when the old man showed up at the township of Maryville. He was an Irishman, burly and quick with a smile and a joke, his hair and whiskers the color of rusty door hinges. No one knew the feller's name, just knew that he toted a pack upon his back full of medicines and notions, and some wooden toys he'd whittled with a sharp blade and a steady hand. There was no general store in Maryville at the time, just a way station that doubled as a tavern and inn. The Peddler, as folks called him, showed up that late December, brimming with songs and stories and a belly big enough to hold his share of beer and bourbon when the menfolk of the village were generous enough to buy him a round or two."

Grandpa paused and eyed his two grandsons. "Now, I ain't boring you, am I? You're not feeling too sleepy to go on, are you?"

"No, sir!" the boys chimed in together.

The elderly man nodded and went on. "Well, it was nigh

on to Christmas Eve, when the Peddler heard tell of a child up in these Tennessee mountains. The boy had fallen beneath a logging wagon and his leg had been shattered, broken in three places. The old peddler was a man of great heart and he felt compassion for the crippled boy. He also learned that the family was hard-hit with poverty. They were dirt-floor poor with scarcely two nickels to rub together."

"So what'd he do, Grandpa?" asked David, although he had heard the story many times before.

"Well, what he did was get out his whittling knife and a slab of white oak and he went to work. The crowd at the tavern grew silent as they watched him carve the most skillfully-crafted figure of a running stallion that they ever did see. It was common knowledge that the lame boy on the mountain was a lover of horses, although he and his family had none to call their own. So the Peddler carved this here toy horse out of wood. Lordy Mercy, they said the little stallion looked so lifelike that it might have galloped across the tabletop with oaken hooves, if the old man had possessed the magic to breathe such life into it.

"Well now, the folks there in the tavern tried to talk the Peddler out of it, but he got it in his head that he should take that toy to the crippled child that very night. It had snowed the majority of the day and it was awful cold outside. But no matter how much they argued with him, the Peddler's heart proved much bigger than his common sense. He bundled up, lifted his pack, and ventured out into the frigid darkness. Having gotten the directions to the boy's cabin from the barkeep, he began his long, dark journey into the foothills, and then onward toward the lofty peaks of the Appalachians."

A German clock on the stone mantelpiece chimed the hour of nine. "Are you sure you young'uns ain't hankering to get to bed? You've had a busy day and you look plumb tuckered out."

"No, sir!" they said, their eyes wide with anticipation. "Please, go on."

Grandpa drew on his pipe again. "Very well...but here is where the spooky part comes along. You see, that peddler got as far as Gimble's Gap and was suddenly trapped in the worse snowstorm the mountains had seen in a month of Sundays.

The blizzard was so cold and icy, and its wind so blustery, that the Peddler couldn't see three feet in front of him. But still he had it in his mind to visit the boy that very night and he trudged onward, through the driving flurries and deep drifts. Somewhere along the way, he lost his bearings. He could have turned back right then and there, and probably made it to the tavern alive. But the Peddler was a stubborn feller and he continued his night's journey through the icy darkness with that wooden horse clutched in one gloved hand. However, the struggle of stepping through the high drifts and the force of the winter wind pushing against him took its toll. It wore him plumb out and slowed him down considerably."

"But he never got there, did he, Grandpa?" asked Chester, although he already knew the answer.

"No, grandson, he never did. His journey up the mountain was in vain. Some of the men from the tavern grew concerned, and the following morning, after the blizzard had subsided, they took off up the mountain, looking for him. On the afternoon of Christmas Day, they found him, frozen to the trunk of a deadfall. They said he was a gruesome sight to behold! His clothing was icy and as hard as stone. His curly red beard was now snowy white, his rosy face was pale and blue, and even his eyeballs were covered over with frost. The old man was dead, having grown exhausted from his treacherous journey and frozen to death on the trunk of that fallen tree."

Grandpa's eyes narrowed a bit, a peculiar look crossing his wrinkled face. "Still and all, there was one strange thing they noticed before they pried his carcass from the log and carried him back down the mountain. The hand that had clutched the wooden horse was empty now...and in the snow, leading away from the dead body of its creator, were the prints of tiny hooves."

Chester and David shuddered in wondrous fright. "So that was the end of the tale?"

"No, by George!" proclaimed Grandpa. "For, you see, every Christmas Eve, the Ghostly Peddler roams the hills and hollows of these here mountains, in search of that wooden horse. The spirit of that stubborn Irishman still has it in his mind to find that wandering pony and give it to its rightful owner...that crippled boy from long years past. But as he makes that lonesome journey, his benevolence still rings as clear as a church bell. He leaves toys, carved by his ghostly hand, in the stockings of the young'uns of these Tennessee mountains, if only for the chance to warm his frozen bones by their midnight fire."

The boys grinned at one another. "Do you think the Peddler will leave us something tonight?" asked David hopefully.

Grandpa tamped out the dregs of his pipe, laid it on the arm of his rocking chair, and stood up. His joints popped as he stretched. "I wouldn't doubt you boys finding a play-pretty in your stockings come daybreak. But he ain't gonna come with you up and about. Best dress for bed and snuggle beneath those covers. He oughta be roaming the mountains on around midnight, looking for that wooden stallion."

Both boys hopped up from the floor, eager to get to sleep. "Goodnight, Grandpa," they said, heading for their parents' room and the little bed they shared there.

"Goodnight, boys," he said, heading for the third room of the cabin and his own bed. "And a very Merry Christmas to you both."

Before long, they had settled into the comfort of a feather mattress, beneath toasty patchwork quilts, and drifted into their separate slumbers. The mountain cabin grew still and quiet. The only sounds to be heard were the crackling of the fire in the hearth and the lonesome howling of a winter wind outside the frosted windowpanes.

A little before midnight, Chester crept from his bed, careful not to rouse his sleeping brother. The story of the Ghostly Peddler was fresh and alive in his mind. Knowing that he really oughtn't do it, he left the bedroom and snuck across the main room, past the hearth. He took up sentry behind his grandfather's high-backed rocker, tucked, unseen, in the shadows just behind.

Chester waited for what seemed to be a very long time. He did not feel the least bit sleepy, though. He crouched there, watching intently, his ears straining for the least little sound. Once or twice, he thought he heard something scamper across the roughly-hewn boards of the plank floor, but knew that it was probably the mouse that had taken up residence there in the cold months prior to Christmas—the rodent who had helped itself to their cornmeal and winter cheese, much to Ma's displeasure.

Finally, the clock chimed the hour of twelve. Chester sat there in breathless anticipation, listening, watching through the pickets of the old rocking chair. He heard a noise in the cabin...the mouse again, he first thought. But, no, it seemed to originate from something a mite larger than a mouse...more like a muskrat or a weasel, perhaps. And the tiny footfalls were odd, too. They sounded more like a small clopping than the skittering of sharply-nailed animal feet upon the floorboards.

For several minutes, Chester sat there. He listened intently, but could hear nothing else. Then, abruptly and without warning, the cabin door burst open. A gust of icy wind, laden with snowflakes as big as goose feathers, blew inside, causing the flames of the hearth to gutter and snap. Then, with the winter's draft, appeared a broad form. He stepped into the cabin and, just as suddenly as before, the pine door closed shut.

Chester's heart thundered in his young chest. There, standing in the center of the main room, was a burly man dressed in icy rags. His broad face was pale blue in color and his hair and beard were covered with frost and jagged icicles. It was the man's eyes that terrified the boy the most. They looked about the room, the orbs frozen and coated with a thin sheen of ice, the pupils barely visible.

So the old stories were true. It was him at last...the Ghostly Peddler!

Chester watched, transfixed in horror, as the spirit crossed the room. He crouched a bit, as though searching the floor for something. That peculiar sound echoed again...the rat or whatever it was.

"I hear ye now," rasped the ghost in a coarse whisper. "Ye'd best not try to hide from me, little one. Your shoeprints have led me to this very door."

Chester wasn't at all sure who the Ghostly Peddler was talking to, until the old man reached between the wood box and his mother's sewing basket and brought something out into the firelight. He watched in utter amazement as the spirit held the tiny creature aloft. It was a small, wooden stallion, bucking and whinnying, as it struggled to escape the icy grasp of the Peddler's gloved hand.

"Gotcha!" laughed the old man in triumph. "After all these years, I'm at journey's end."

Chester watched as the ghost walked to the stone hearth. It was there that an incredible transformation took place. The old peddler stood before the glow of the crackling flames, seeming to drink in its golden warmth. The icy exterior of the apparition slowly melted away, revealing a robust Irishman wearing a worn tweed suitcoat, britches, walking boots, and a brown derby hat. His face grew rosy, his beard its true color of rusty redness, and his eyes sparkled a brilliant hazel green. A grin crossed his ruddy face and he sighed contentedly.

"'Tis grand to be amongst the living again," he said aloud. "If only for a wee time."

Chester watched as the Peddler set the wooden stallion on the stone mantle. The tiny horse reared defiantly, flashing its small hooves and snorting in frustration. Then it trotted to and fro, down one end of the stone ledge to the other. The old man opened his leather pack and took several wooden toys from inside: a top, building blocks, a couple of soldiers brandishing muskets and cavalry swords. He deposited them in the boys' stockings, nodding to himself in satisfaction.

When he spoke again, he spoke not to himself, but to Chester. "I know you're there, lad," he said. "Peering at me from behind the chair. Come here, will ye? I wish to entrust a very special gift unto your care."

Curiously, Chester stood up and walked toward the hearth. Strangely enough, he was not frightened by the ghostly Irishman who stood before the fire. When he came within six feet of the old man, the Peddler took the horse from the mantle and extended it to him. "See to it that young Johnny receives this present, will ye not? I meant for him to have it a very long time ago...but, alas, the journey here was much farther than I could have ever imagined."

"Yes, sir," muttered Chester. He reached out for the stallion, but it whinnied and snapped at him with its tiny oaken teeth.

"Go on. Take it now. It'll not harm ye, boy."

Chester took hold of the squirming animal, and the moment his fingertips touched it, the stallion became no more than a wooden toy again.

"I'm much obliged to ye," said the Peddler with a courteous tip of his bowler.

Chester stepped back a few feet and watched as the ghost closed his eyes, breathed deeply, and beamed a great smile. "My work here is done," he said softly. "Dear Father, take me hither to me heavenly home." Then his burly form grew as bright and brilliant as a white-hot horseshoe in a blacksmith's forge. The Peddler seemed to dissolve into a thousand fiery cinders, which swirled about the cabin for a frantic moment, then flew up the dark channel of the stone chimney and skyward into the snowy night.

Chester stood there for a moment, dazed. He looked down at his flannel nightshirt and his bare feet and wondered if it had only been a dream...that perhaps he had merely been sleepwalking. But then he looked at the stockings filled with toys and the wooden stallion in his hand and he knew for a fact that it had all taken place.

He heard movement behind him and turned to find Grandpa standing there in the doorway of his bedroom. "What's going on?" asked the elderly man drowsily. "I thought I heard voices."

Chester smiled, his eyes livid with excitement. "You did," he replied. He held the wooden horse out to his grandfather. "I was told to give this to you...or, rather, to young Johnny."

With a trembling hand, Grandpa took the toy, his eyes brimming with youthful wonder. "So he finally made it," he said. "After all these years."

Chester watched as John McCorkendale gently cradled the wooden stallion with the reverence of some great and long sought-after treasure. Then, limping, the old man returned to the comfort of his bed...and boyish dreams of decades long past.

ABOUT THE AUTHOR

Ronald Kelly was born November 20, 1959 in Nashville, Tennessee. He attended Pegram Elementary School and Cheatham County Central High School before starting his writing career.

Ronald Kelly began his writing career in 1986 and quickly sold his first short story, "Breakfast Serial," to *Terror Time Again* magazine. His first novel, *Hindsight* was released by Zebra Books in 1990. His audiobook collection, *Dark Dixie: Tales of Southern Horror*, was on the nominating ballot of the 1992 Grammy Awards for Best Spoken Word or Non-Musical Album. Zebra published eight of Ronald Kelly's novels from 1990 to 1996. Ronald's short fiction work has been published by *Cemetery Dance, Borderlands 3, Deathrealm, Dark at Heart, Hot Blood: Seeds of Fear*, and many more. After selling hundreds of thousands of books, the bottom dropped out of the horror market in 1996. So, when Zebra dropped their horror line in October 1996, Ronald Kelly stopped writing for almost ten years and worked various jobs including welder, factory worker, production manager, drugstore manager, and custodian.

In 2006, Ronald Kelly started writing again. In early 2008, Croatoan Publishing released his work *Flesh Welder* as a standalone chapbook, and it quickly sold out. In early 2009 Cemetery Dance Publications released a limited edition hardcover of his first short story collection, *Midnight Grinding & Other Twilight Terrors*. Also in 2010, Cemetery Dance released his first novel in over ten years called, *Hell Hollow* as a limited edition hardcover. Ronald's Zebra/Pinnacle horror novels were released by Thunderstorm Books as The Essential Ronald Kelly series. Each book contains a new novella related to the novel's original storyline. His eBooks and audiobooks are with Crossroad Press.

Ronald Kelly currently lives in a backwoods hollow in Brush Creek, Tennessee, with his wife, Joyce, and their three children.

Curious about other Crossroad Press books?
Stop by our site:
http://store.crossroadpress.com
We offer quality writing
in digital, audio, and print formats.

Made in the USA
Las Vegas, NV
22 October 2023

79463032R10080